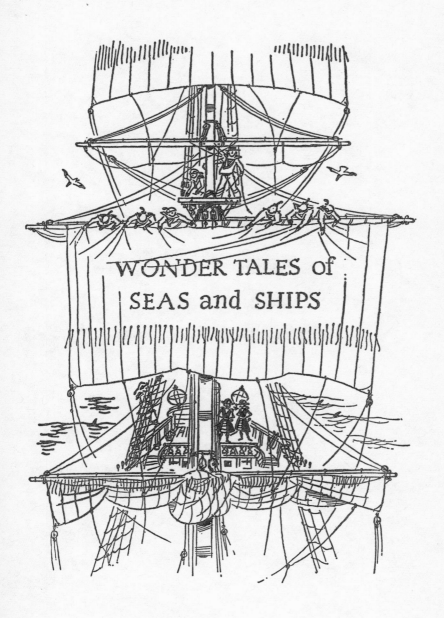

WONDER TALES of
SEAS and SHIPS

By Frances Carpenter

WONDER TALES
of
SEAS and SHIPS
by Frances Carpenter

illustrated by
Peter Spier

Design: Charles Kaplan

Library of Congress Catalog Card Number 59–12619
Copyright © 1959 by Frances Carpenter Huntington
All Rights Reserved. First Edition
Printed in the United States of America
First Edition

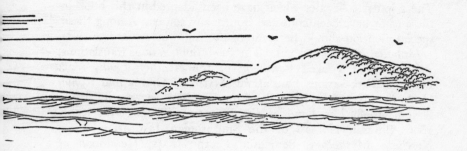

TO CHAPIN

with whom I have sailed many seas

The popular folk tales which have been adapted in this book by the author have been collected from many sources. Among these, special mention should be made of the following:

Alphabetum Siracidis, 1514; *The Ramayana*, various translations, 2d cent. B.C.; Tooke's *Pantheon of the Heathen Gods*, 1825; Homer's *Iliad*, various translations; *Myths of Greece and Rome*, H. A. Guerber, 1907; *Legends of the Filipinos*, Margherita Arlina Hamm, 1898; *The Land of the Kangaroo*, Thomas W. Knox, 1896; Bulletin No. 18 of the Smithsonian Institution, 1897; *Northern Mythology*, Benjamin Thorpe, 1841; *Handbook of Legendary and Mythological Art*, Clara Erskine Clement, 1877; *Légendes de la Mer*, P. Sébillot, 1896; *Turi's Book of Lapland*, Johan Turi, 1910; *The Algonquin Legends of New England*, Charles G. Leland, 1884; *Myths of the Norsemen*, H. A. Guerber, 1908; *Myths of Ancient Egypt*, Lewis Spence, 1915; *Superstitions of Sailors*, Dr. Angelo S. Rappoport, 1928; *Folklore Chilien*, G. et J. Soustelle, 1938; *Myths and Legends of China*, E. T. C. Werner, 1922; "Shark Beliefs," article in the *Hawaiian Annual*, 1923; *Le Livre des Vikings*, Ch. Guyot et E. Wegener, 1924; the arctic writings of Vilhjalmur Stefansson and K. J. V. Rasmussen.

Acknowledgments

CONTENTS

Contents

[10]

Contents

[11]

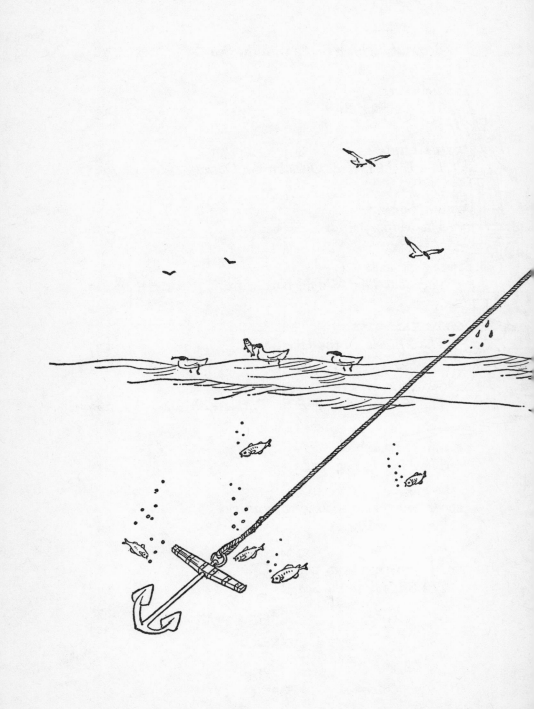

Anchors aweigh........

The Sailor and
The Sea Serpent

*T*o the oars! bend to the oars!"

At this shout from the Captain, the Egyptian boy, Inteb, ran to the side of his father's fat sailing ship. He took care not to bump against the bundles that were piled high inside this gaily painted wood vessel of long, long ago.

The rolls of straw matting held the ship's precious cargo. Fine Egyptian linens, bales of white cotton, and creamy elephant-ivory tusks from far up the River Nile lay there on the ship's bottom. Inteb could smell the sweet oils and the fragrant myrrh which would bring such high prices in the towns along the shores of the ancient Mediterranean Sea.

Above the ship's bow, the signal flag was flying in the strong breeze. And at the order from the Captain, the rowing song of the oarsmen began. Inteb liked the smooth swing of their long oaken blades. Together, as one, the row of oars on each side of the ship dipped in and out, in and out of the River Nile.

The boy's heart beat fast with excitement. This was to be his first journey out upon the Mediterranean Sea. He had, of course, often traveled up and down the Nile River on the boats of his father, the rich trader, Esar. But on this day he was beginning a voyage which would take him out through the muddy mouth of the river. It would bring him onto the wide blue waters of the sea itself.

Secretly, Inteb was a little afraid of this sea. He well knew its dangers. Too many times he had heard of its demons, which ride on stormy waves to do mischief to ships. But the boy gave no sign of his fear that day when he ran to join his father in the bow of the vessel.

"Did you remember your scarab, Inteb, my son?" Esar looked fondly down at the boy.

"But surely, my father," Inteb cried happily. "How should I forget my scarab which protects me from harm? Surely, we shall need its help, too, during our journey. See, I have it here, safe inside my belt. And I have rubbed it with sweet oil."

The Egyptian boy unwrapped the tiny packet of fine linen. Between his thumb and his forefinger he held up for his father to see, a bit of shining red stone carved in the shape of a beetle. To Inteb, his scarab was like a guardian angel or a small god.

"Aye, we shall need its help, my son!" The trader spoke in a solemn tone. "Blessed be our scarabs! And blessed be the great God of the Sea! May he listen well to our prayers for safety upon his waves!"

The ship now was moving slowly, pulled by its oarsmen through the muddy mouth of the Nile. The rich shipowner, Esar, his Captain, and all the crew who were not bent to the oars now bowed very low. In singsong voices they sent out over the waves their prayers to the unseen spirit ruler of the watery world they were entering.

When their prayers had been chanted, Esar called to the Captain, "The wind blows fair. The sail now can be spread."

In silence, Esar and Inteb watched the giant square of heavy red-brown linen slide along the tall cedar mast.

"Our ship has a good mast, my son." Esar looked proudly at the strong pole. "Its wood came from the faraway forests of Lebanon, where trees grow so tall that they kiss the sky. From the Land of Bashan came our ship's timbers. O, it is safe in the highest waves which the sea demons throw against it."

"Our ship may not be the biggest ship on the sea, my father," Inteb replied, "but surely it is the most beautiful."

The boy was looking at the handsome wood figure mounted upon the bow of the vessel. It was the splendid image of a sea god, cleverly carved to show a man's body with a fish's tail.

The two great round staring eyes, painted on either side of the ship's bow, made Inteb feel safe. "With such big eyes," he thought, "our ship can surely find its way safely over the sea. Even when clouds hide the stars from Kebo, the steersman, those eyes can see where we should go."

Inteb's journey out upon the Mediterranean Sea took place long, long ago, even before Christ was born. In those days a ship's compass and the steering instruments of to-day had not even been dreamed of. The stars then were the best guides for men on the sea.

The shipowner's son liked to squat beside Kebo, the steersman. Kebo was a Phoenician. From his Syrian land of Phoenicia came some of the most splendid ships of early times. In the ancient Mediterranean world, Phoenician traders and seamen were famous.

When the wind was fair, Kebo needed only one hand to guide the paddle rudder which kept the ship on its path. The vessel sped along smoothly, almost by itself. The steersman could then make himself comfortable and tell Inteb strange tales he had heard during his wanderings over the sea.

The story Inteb liked best was the one about a lucky sailor and the sea-serpent god, Ka.

This lucky sailor was an oarsman on a fine Egyptian vessel. Its one hundred boatmen were strong. Yet in spite of this, that fine ship was broken to pieces by the sea demons in the midst of a storm.

"Only one sailor was saved," Kebo told Inteb. "That one must have had a powerful scarab. Or he must have found favor in the eyes of the Sea God. For great good luck came to him.

"As he struggled in the high waves, a wooden beam from the broken ship floated right under his arms. He could cling fast to it and ride safely over that stormy sea.

"For many days this sailor and his sturdy beam were tossed about by the waves. And then at last, one morning, they were washed up on the shores of a fine, fair green island.

"The island's sandy beach was dry, and soft to sleep upon." Kebo nodded his head. He seemed to understand just how the shipwrecked sailor had felt. It was almost as though he himself had, more than once, been saved from the sea.

"When the sailor had rested, he looked about him for food. On that fine, fair green island he found ripe berries, sweet figs, and juicy grapes. In the waves that rolled up to his feet there were fish for the taking. From the air came fat birds to give him fresh meat. Yet, before he put even one morsel of food into his mouth, he made a thank-offering to the God of the Sea, who had saved him from the storm demons.

"The next day," Kebo, the steersman, went on with the tale, "a clap of loud thunder roared over the sailor's head. 'Another tempest! Alas!' the sailor cried aloud. He looked fearfully upward, expecting to see the heavy black storm clouds. But the sky was as blue and as clear as on a bright summer day.

"Still the winds blew!" Kebo now made a shrill whistling sound. "The trees on the island bowed their heads to the ground. The earth beneath the sailor's feet shook like a leaf in a breeze. And, out of the waves, up onto the shore, there crawled a monster sea serpent.

"Now, Inteb, my boy, many a sailor has seen a sea serpent. I have seen two myself," Kebo declared, nodding his head. "But usually sea serpents appear off at a distance. They rush through the waves so swiftly that all one can follow are their coils, which seem like dark little islands sticking out of the water. This serpent was as close to that sailor as I am to you, Inteb." The steersman nodded his head again when he told of this wonder.

"A monster serpent it truly was," Kebo continued. "Its giant body had the blue and green colors of the deep sea. Its scales shone like the gold of the setting sun. And its beard was as long as your arm."

"Wasn't that sailor afraid, Kebo?" Inteb broke in, as he saw with his mind's eye the terrible sight.

"He was frozen with fear," Kebo replied. "That shipwrecked sailor threw himself down at the feet of the sea monster. Not daring to look up at the creature's fierce open jaws, he hid his face in the sand.

"'Well, Man, what are you doing here on my fine, fair green island?' The sea serpent's angry words brought fresh terror to the frightened sailor's heart.

"'A demon wrecked our ship, Mighty One,' the trembling fellow found courage, at last, to reply. 'The storm sent by that demon broke our strong ship to pieces. Of its one hundred boatmen, only I was not lost in the high stormy waves. Surely it was some good Sea God who brought me safe to this place.

" 'I would gladly go away, O Serpent!' the sailor added quickly. 'Gladly, O gladly would I return to my own land of Egypt!'

"This sailor pleased the sea serpent. The monster now spoke more gently. 'You shall go back to your home, Sailor,' he said. 'A ship of your ruler, of the Pharaoh himself, shall come here to fetch you. I, Ka, God of the Sea, say it shall be so. And when you once more are in Egypt, you shall tell that Pharaoh how fine and how fair is the green Island of Ka.'

"Well, each day on Ka's Island, the sailor climbed into the treetops to look for the Pharaoh's ship that should come to take him away. And at last one day it appeared as the Sea God, Ka, had foretold." Kebo sighed with relief as he told this part of the tale.

"Ka and his seventy-five sea-serpent brothers loaded that vessel with rich gifts for the Pharaoh. Piled in it were sweet-smelling woods and rare spices, perfumes and ivory, and even small apes for the amusement of the Egyptian King.

"What a welcome that shipwrecked sailor received at the court of the Pharaoh!" Kebo exclaimed. "How astonished were all at the tale of his strange adventure!

"Other sailors wished to set forth at once to find that fine, fair green Island of Ka. But the shipwrecked one told them the island had disappeared from the sea the moment he set foot on the ship of the Pharaoh.

" 'Lucky art thou, O Sailor,' the Pharaoh exclaimed when the tale was told. 'Never before has any man set foot on the Island of Ka. And it may well be that no man will ever find it again. The Great Ka has protected you. Every sea captain will want you and your luck aboard his ship. Fortune surely rides with you.'

"And so it was, Inteb. Of all the sailors on our Great Sea in those times, that shipwrecked sailor was luckiest."

When Kebo, the steersman, ended his story, the eyes of his young friend were filled with wonder. This Egyptian boy of so long ago believed in wicked demons and powerful gods. He was sure storms were sent by demons of the sea. And without help from his scarab and other Egyptian gods, he surely would drown.

In those ancient times the true causes of the sea's wonders had not even been dreamed of. How then could people like Esar or Kebo explain the mysteries of the ocean except as the work of beings with magic power?

Across the pages of this book there march many strange creatures, quite as strange as the sea serpent whose name was the Great Ka. These beings were invented by sailors of ancient times to explain happenings which they themselves could not understand.

Witches that rode on the winds! Saints who protected sailors from the tempest! Sea kings and sea princesses in fabulous undersea palaces! We know such creatures are found only in folk tales. But on the other hand, we can be sure that, so long ago, when these stories first were told, boys like Inteb really believed they could be true.

The Frog That Swallowed
the Ocean

*W*HAT DO YOU SEE WHEN YOU LOOK AT THE FULL MOON?

Do you see a man's face in the dark shadows on its round shining face? Is it a Moon Rabbit like the one in the old Chinese fairy tales? Or can you make out the shape of the giant frog which, in many an ancient land, was thought to live in the moon?

It was a frog that Yokkai, the Australian bush boy, was trying to see one night long, long ago. In his ancient times there were many, many more of his dark-skinned people on the continent of Australia than there are today.

The Australian bush people were wild, as wild as the tangled bush country where they roamed with their hunting spears. Some were cannibals. People say these bushmen were more like the cave dwellers of earliest times than any people on earth.

On that long-ago night when the boy Yokkai squatted by the village campfire, his people believed firmly in magic. They had no doubt that there was a giant frog in the moon. They thought the story of how he once drank up the ocean could easily be true.

Yokkai's old grandfather was telling this story that night by the campfire. The full moon shone down on his dark brown wrinkled face. In its pale light his teeth and his bone nosepins gleamed white against his dark face. The bush people who were gathered around him could see his eyes shine as he told the tale I set down here for you.

"It was Bayamey, God-who-made-the-world," the old bushman began his tale. "It was Bayamey who spread the wide waters out here, far below his blue sky. Bayamey lifted the earth up from under the sea. And he was pleased with his work.

"'You, Earth, shall be covered with green plants and grass,' Bayamey cried. 'You shall be covered with flowers and trees. Birds shall sit upon the tree branches. Honey-bees shall light on the flowers. And kangaroos and other wild creatures, good for man to eat, shall roam over the land.'"

The old bushman's voice rose high and shrill as he told what a good world Bayamey was making.

"Then Bayamey turned his face to the ocean," the old man continued. "'Your bed, O Ocean, shall cover more of this world than does the land,' he said. 'Wide shall be your waters. Great shall be your strength. Loud shall be the voice of your waves when they break on the shore.

"'But take care, O Ocean! Take care that you stay in your own part of my world. Do not let your waters roll out of your bed. Never, no, never must you spread far over the earth. Have you understood me? Do you promise to obey?'"

The storyteller's voice grew so loud and so angry that Yokkai trembled. It was almost as though he were hearing the voice of God himself.

"'I will obey, my Master,' the ocean replied. And for a time the earth and the ocean dwelt together in peace." Yokkai's old grandfather spoke more softly now.

"Of course the ocean waves broke on the shore and their voices were loud. But their waters quickly rolled back again where they belonged.

"In time, however, the ocean grew too proud of its power and strength. It raised its waves higher and higher. Farther and farther its great rollers came crashing up onto the land. Flowers and trees were spoiled by the sea water. Land creatures had to run back, back into the forests. They climbed up on the rocks and into the treetops so as not to be drowned. And they complained to Bayamey, God-who-made-the-world.

"Bayamey himself came down from the sky." Again the tone of the old bushman's voice warned of trouble. "'Wicked Ocean, Bayamey is angry.' The God's voice was like thunder. 'You have not kept your promise. You have not obeyed my command. You were not content that you should own more of the world than I gave to the earth. You thought you were stronger than the One-who-made-you. I shall teach you a lesson.'

"'All of your water, and all the waters that feed you, shall disappear from my world. And they shall not come back again, until I have forgotten my anger.' These were the terrible words spoken by Bayamey."

Yokkai's eyes opened wide with wonder when his grandfather told of the giant frog which came down out of the sky. And how it sucked up the vast ocean out of its bed. Of course it was Bayamey himself. By his magic he had changed himself into the frog. No doubt he was the very same frog which the boy now thought he could see on the moon.

What would a world be without water? Yokkai said to himself. How could plants grow? How could men drink? What would become of the fish in the sea or the thirsty animals on the land?

"Was there no water at all in the world then, Grandfather?" Yokkai asked, wondering.

"How can I say, Boy? I was not there. There may have been some left in the brooks and the streams. Or it may be that Bayamey kept the fish and the animals and the birds alive with his magic. But he said the ocean should have no more water. And surely there was none."

The bush grandfather then told how all the animals gathered together on the dry beach. The fishes were there, and the birds, too. They talked and they talked of how they could get Bayamey to forget his anger and let the ocean waters come back to the world.

" 'Our waters are in the stomach of the giant frog which came down to earth from the moon.' It was an "old-man" kangaroo who spoke. He was an ancient beast, and the animals listened to his words.

" 'I can see the frog in the moon clearly, and he keeps his lips tight shut.' This was from a beady-eyed koala bear in a treetop. This furry little beast was not really interested in water to drink. He always quenched his thirst on the juicy leaves of the eucalyptus tree. But he wanted to be helpful.

"The animals and the birds and the fishes peered up into the night sky. As clear as the round shape of the moon, they could see the giant frog outlined on its bright disk."

As the storyteller paused for a moment, all the bush people turned their eyes on the moon above them. They, too, could see the frog there, or so they thought.

" 'Surely that frog is Bayamey. If we can make the frog laugh, its anger will be forgotten. The frog will open his mouth when he laughs, and the ocean waters will come forth.' " This was the happy idea of a kookooburra bird. Who should know better about laughing than he? His loud ha-ha-ha could be heard all through the forests of Australia.

" 'Yes, we must make the frog laugh.' The animals and the fishes and the birds cried out in a chorus." The bushman nodded his head. He thought this was a fine idea.

[33]

"'I will try first,' the kookooburra offered. 'I will laugh and laugh. Perhaps the frog will join in.'"

And up from that sandy beach, so the story went, there rose the cry of this big-headed brown bird. In some other lands the kookooburra is called the "laughing jackass," and truly its sharp cry is much like a donkey's bray.

"Ha-ha-ha! Hoo-hoo-hoo!" The call of that kookooburra bird was so loud that it surely must have reached the moon.

No doubt the giant frog heard it. But he made no sign. He only blinked his round eyes. His thin lips remained shut.

"I can laugh louder than that," the dingo dog boasted. He opened his jaws and howled up at the moon. Still the face of the frog did not change.

"One after the other, the animals and the birds, and the fishes, too, tried to make that frog laugh." The storyteller shook his head as he described the antics each one performed there on the Australian beach so long ago.

He told how the young kangaroos stood up, tall on their strong tails. Others of these giant "hoppers" chased one another in high bounds over the bushes. But that did not seem funny at all to the frog in the moon. He was used to looking down upon kangaroos jumping about.

The blue-satin bowerbird, which dances so clumsily for its mate, went through its paces. And a tortoise stuck out its scrawny head towards the moon and danced along behind on its short little legs.

[34]

Surely this should make the frog in the moon laugh. But it did not. The creature's wide lips were shut in a thin line. No water could get through them.

A whale stood on its tail and smiled at the moon. Two bottle-nosed dolphins turned somersaults on the dry bed of the sea. Alas, it was no use.

"Let us try, too," cried two long, thin eels, wriggling forward. "Let us also dance for the frog in the moon, that his anger may be forgotten."

Never had there been such turning and twisting. The eel's long snake-like bodies glided this way and that way. And then, by some lucky chance, the two slimy creatures tied themselves together into a knot. They tied that knot so well that they could not undo it.

"All the animals laughed. The fishes laughed, too. And so did the birds and the honeybees." The old grandfather began to laugh, himself, as he told this part of the tale. "And while all the creatures were laughing at the two eels trying to untangle themselves, there came a cry from the top of the eucalyptus tree.

" 'The great frog is smiling now.' It was the koala bear calling. 'Look! Look! The frog in the moon is about to laugh.'

"With a sound like thunder, the frog's first laugh rolled over the beach. His wide mouth stretched open in an enormous guffaw. His anger was forgotten!

"The waters of the thirsty world came pouring out of

the frog's open mouth. In torrents they fell. And the land creatures would all have been drowned if the pelican had not scooped them into the safety of his huge beak."

The old bushman smiled at the happy ending to his tale.

"The ocean once more lay sparkling in its own bed. Clear water filled the streams that flow through the land. Lakes and ponds were full too. And all creatures rejoiced."

"Never again did Bayamey have to punish the ocean." Now the story was coming to its close. "Sometimes, today, the big waves try to roll up over the land. But the ocean pulls them back so quickly that Bayamey does not have time to grow angry."

"And the frog we see in the moon, Grandfather?" Yokkai asked when the story was told. "Is that one the same frog who put the ocean back in its place so long ago?"

"Who knows, Boy?" was the old bushman's reply. "People say it is the moon frog, sucking away at the ocean, which causes low water. Then he thinks of the two eels and he laughs again, so that the water rises high again. That is the way it could be, I think."

Yokkai liked his grandfather's story. Next day the boy drew a huge frog on the wall of a cave not far from his village camp. With the strong colors his people made, he showed the blue water pouring out of the creature's laughing mouth. He put two yellow eels, all twisted together, not far away, and an "old-man" kangaroo and a kookooburra bird nearby, looking on.

[36]

The Angakok
and the Mother
of Seals

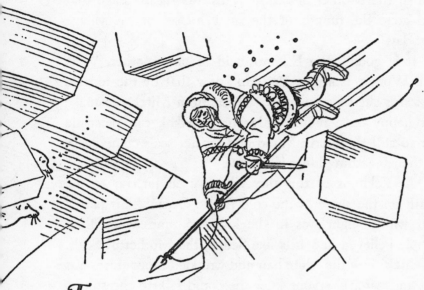

THE SINGING HOUSE OF THE ESKIMO VILLAGE WAS
crowded. All the thirty people of the igloos were gathered
in this big snow lodge which they had built for their dancing and singing.

The older women sat at the back, close to the curved
snow wall of the igloo. The younger women and their
children made up the middle circle. And in the very front,
of course, were the Eskimo men.

But the men, too, had pushed themselves back so as to
leave an open space in the center for Old Mitek. He was
their Wise Man, their Angakok. And all eyes were upon
him.

"Tonight Mitek will go down under the sea to find

Sedna, the Mother of Seals." This was the message that had gone the rounds of the snow houses of the village that day.

"It is good!" the Eskimos said to one another. "The Seal Woman is angry. We can know that by the terrible blizzards she sends us. Only a visit from Mitek can make her happy once more. Only our Angakok can persuade her to still the North Wind and let her seals come again to their breathing holes in the ice."

The Eskimos of this tiny village lived far, far to the north on the shore of the cold Arctic Ocean. This particular winter night was in the long-ago times when their people believed in spirits like Sedna, the Mother of Seals.

Mitek, with the white hair and wrinkled brown face, was old and wise. Everyone knew he could talk to the spirits. With his charms and his chants, he could cure sickness. That is how it was that he had become their Medicine Man, or, as the Eskimos called him, their Angakok.

It was hot inside the Singing House. Oily heat rose from the soapstone lamps on the little shelves cut into the snow walls. More warmth came from so many people crowded together in the airless igloo. Most of the men and women had thrown off their furry caribou-skin parkas. But, even so, drops of perspiration stood out on their tawny shoulders.

Mitek stood in the very center of the igloo, not far from the smoke hole in its rounded roof. His only garments were his short caribou-skin trousers and his bearskin boots.

The Angakok and the Mother of Seals

Of course, he still wore his Angakok's seal-hide belt with its magic charms. The children, especially a bright-eyed boy named Papik, counted these charms to make sure all were there. The caribou tooth, the raven's claw, the tiny model of a kayak, and a bit of carved walrus ivory—Papik knew them by heart.

The journey which Old Mitek was about to make to the undersea home of the Mother of Seals was important to all in the Singing House. The caribou meat from the summer hunting, now, was almost gone. Great blizzards had kept the hunters from going out to the seals' breathing holes with their harpoons. Even on days when they dared brave the weather, they came home empty-handed.

Everyone in that northern village was hungry. There was no doubt but that Sedna was angry. Why else would she keep all her seals from coming to the breathing holes?

Now it was the dark of the moon. There was not even a faint glow in the sky. The time was right for Old Mitek to make his visit to Sedna, the Mother of Seals.

"I'm ready now. Bind my arms and my legs!" The Angakok was squatting down in the center of the open space. Two young Eskimo hunters stepped forward. With long strips of sealhide they tied his arms and his legs so that he could not possibly rise from the snow floor of the Singing House.

"Put out the lamps! All eyes must be closed!" The Angakok's voice was loud.

Everyone obeyed his command. That is, everyone but

the boy Papik. That one opened his narrow eyes for just one last look. But the room was so dark that he could see nothing. And before his eyes could become used to the darkness, the boy felt a hand slide gently across his eyes. It was the hand of his mother, he knew. She was not going to risk her son's being hurt by the magic of the Angakok, who would be angry if he should peek.

In the Singing House not a sound was to be heard except the breathing of the excited Eskimos. Then Old Mitek, the Angakok, began to speak in a low singsong voice.

"Ha-la-la! Ha-la-le! Ha-la-la! Ha-la-le!" he chanted. "My body grows light. Light as a little bird's feather, it is. Like a dry stick on the ocean, it floats, O it floats."

The old man's voice seemed to come now from under the top of the Singing House. Papik knew Old Mitek must still be sitting where he had been tied on the snow floor. But then, what could it be that was whirling and whizzing around the igloo? Surely it had to be the Angakok's spirit rising into the air.

"I fly like a bird up over your heads. Now, out the smoke hole I go. Ha-la-la! Ha-la-le!" The Angakok's voice was growing fainter. The other Eskimos could scarcely hear his last words, "My guardian spirit is leading the way to the home of the Seal Woman."

The whizzing noise now was gone. For a few moments there was only silence in the darkness of the Singing House. Then, to make the waiting easier, someone began to sing softly. It was a song about Sedna which everyone knew, and all joined in the singing.

The song told the sad story of the Mother of Seals. How once she had been a human girl! How she had refused to marry the old man her father had chosen for her husband! And how, instead, she became the bride of a handsome young hunter whom she loved well.

In those times animal creatures, it was said, could take on the form of human beings. And this young hunter, in truth, was the wild seabird known as a petrel.

It is not strange that Sedna's father should have been angry. Nor that he should have gone after her. But he need not have been so cruel. He snatched her away from her beloved young husband. And he threw her into his boat.

Hardly had the man paddled away from the shore when black storm clouds hid the sky. Winds blew the waves up into mountains of dark water.

"Turn back to the shore, Father!" Sedna cried out. "My husband is angry. He will upset your boat. He is no ordinary man, but a sea petrel in a man's form. And he rides on the storm."

The father was trying with all his might to keep his boat right side up. But he looked up at the dark sky, and there in the racing clouds he saw a giant petrel flapping its long wings over his head.

"Unlucky girl," he screamed at Sedna, who crouched at his feet. "Because of you my boat will be lost, and I will be lost too. But your petrel shall never have you." And with that, the cruel man threw his daughter out of his canoe into the foaming waves.

Sedna caught hold of the edge of the boat. There she clung fast, lest she be drowned.

"Let go, girl! Let go!" Her father tried to loosen her hold on his boat. And when she would not—— O, this is the part of the song's story which Papik found hard to believe. His people all loved their children. But the father of Sedna, so the song ran, brought the sharp edge of his paddle down on her clinging fingers. Again and again the sharp edge of the paddle fell on her hands until it had cut off all her fingers.

The girl's finger joints fell down, down into the ocean. Papik and his people sang about how each little finger joint turned into a seal.

Sedna herself floated safely to the sea bottom. It was there she still lived, so Papik thought. And from her open-roofed igloo she ruled all the seals which had been made from her fingers.

It was not hard for Papik to believe that the heroine of this fairy tale could bring forth a blizzard. Had she not been the wife of a stormy petrel?

He could understand also why Sedna should have power over the seals in the ocean. They were her children and her children's children.

The boy was thinking of these things when suddenly he heard old Mitek's voice again. It sounded as if it came from far, far away.

"I am floating in through the smoke hole." The voice

was louder now. "I have returned from the sea bottom. The lamps may be lit."

In the smoky light of the seal-oil lamps, Papik could see that the old man's arms and legs were still tied with the hide straps. It did not seem strange to him that no drop of sea water clung to his trousers or boots. Because it was only the Angakok's spirit that had gone down under the waves.

"I found Sedna in her igloo." The Angakok stood up and stretched his arms high over his head. "I broke down the guard wall around it. And I did not let the Seal Woman's fierce dog stop me from going inside.

"There Sedna sat, with her seals crowded around her. Her back was turned toward me. And I could see her long hair, dirty and tangled, hanging over her shoulders. In a sad state she was. And angry, too. Her face was as dark as the storm clouds of a blizzard."

Every woman and girl in that Singing House cried softly, "Ah! Ah!" They were sorry for Sedna, who, without any fingers, could not get the shells and the sand and the tangles out of her hair. They held their breath until the Angakok told how he had turned the Seal Woman around to face him. How he had gently taken the seaweed out of her hair with his own fingers! And how, when he had smoothed it, she had smiled and made him a feast of seal liver.

"One by one, Sedna pushed the seals out of her igloo." Mitek's voice was triumphant. "Tomorrow there will be seals at the breathing holes. Tomorrow we shall have good hunting weather. For when Sedna smiles, no icy blizzard will come."

Papik wondered how the Angakok could have traveled so far and done so much in such a short time. Then he remembered that the old man had told him that time under the sea was not at all like time on the land. A few minutes of earth time could be many hours on the floor of the ocean.

It was easy for this Eskimo boy to believe the Angakok's story. He himself had been in the Singing House when the old man's spirit went out of the smoke hole. He had heard with his own ears the same whizzing noise when it floated back. And Mitek, who had been there, told just how it was in the undersea home of Sedna, Mother of Seals.

No one could deny that the next day's weather was good. Nor that the seals again came to their breathing holes in the frozen ocean.

Pelops and Poseidon

*T*HE SKY OVERHEAD WAS AS BLUE AS THE SEA THAT washed the shores of ancient Greece. The sun's rays fell full on the white pillars of the nearby temple of Poseidon, the great God of the Sea. Its bright light almost hurt the eyes of the boy Milo, who sat beside his father, Arion, on a stone seat in the hippodrome.

Hundreds of men and boys were crowded together on the rising circles of seats in this open-air theater outside the Greek city of Corinth. From near and far they had come to watch the great games being held there to honor Poseidon.

The time was long, long ago. The Greeks then still believed in the magic of their powerful gods upon lofty Mount Olympus. They said the mightiest of all these gods,

[49]

Zeus, ruled the earth. Poseidon, brother of Zeus, was their God of the Sea.

Poseidon, they thought, called forth the raging tempests which could overturn their ships. He could calm the stormiest waves. And he could shake the earth with his trident, his long shining spear with its three slender sharp points.

The sea was important to these ancient Greeks. Upon it their ships traveled and traded. Its fish gave them food. Their comfortable lives, indeed, depended on the sea.

"It is good that we honor Poseidon here," Arion said to his son that day. "Poseidon will enjoy watching these games from Mount Olympus, I know. Especially the chariot races will please him, since he was the god who created the first horse."

Milo knew well how Poseidon had given the horse to man. He often wished he had been there to see the god strike the earth with his trident, and the splendid horse leap out of the opening which it made in the ground.

Poseidon was Milo's favorite among all the heavenly beings upon Mount Olympus. Often the boy gazed across the wide blue sea, hoping to see this god ride forth from his other palace down under the waves.

The god's chariot would be drawn by two magnificent sea horses, each one with two prancing forefeet and a great fish's tail. The sea would be calm, and its waters would part to let Poseidon's golden car roll, dry, along the sea bottom. But, of course, being a mere mortal, Milo never did see this splendid sight.

[50]

From his high seat there in the oval hippodrome, Milo had a clear view of the games taking place in the arena below. The young runners were swift. The wrestlers were strong. The discus throwers sent their round weights flying far through the air.

But the chariot races were even more exciting. With their manes flying, and their small ears held back tight against their noble heads, the galloping horses went like the wind. The light chariots they drew whirled from one side to another. O, these races were the best of all the contests that honored the great Sea God, Poseidon.

"Now comes the race of Pelops. Watch for the crash, my son!" Arion rose to his feet with the rest of the crowd. Milo jumped up onto the stone seat. He did not want to miss the wreck of the chariot as it rounded the curve. Its wheels would roll off. Its driver would be spilled out. It would only be the magic of Poseidon that could save the charioteer from being killed.

This part of the games was not a true race. It was really a play that showed how Poseidon once helped his young nephew, Pelops, to win his fair bride.

The story of Pelops and Poseidon was well known in ancient Greece. As it was told to boys and girls of those long-ago times, I will tell it to you.

A war had driven brave Pelops out of his Greek kingdom of Lydia. With ships filled with his treasures, the handsome young Prince had crossed the Aegean Sea. In other parts of Greece he would set up a new kingdom for himself. He would, he hoped, marry the beautiful Greek Princess, Hippodameia, with whom he had long been in love.

Hippodameia was as fair as Aphrodite, the Goddess of Beauty and Love. So it was not at all strange that many princes like Pelops wanted her for their bride.

King Oenomaus, the father of this fair Princess, however, did not want her to marry. Some said it was because he loved his daughter so much that he could not bear the thought of her ever leaving his palace.

Others said it was because of the Oracle, the voice of the gods which came from the farthest depths of a cave.

"When his daughter finds a husband, Oenomaus shall meet his death." This was the warning which the priest of the Oracle had given that King.

So Oenomaus sent forth, over the land and the sea, a warning to suitors who might ask to wed Hippodameia.

"He who marries my daughter must first win over me in a chariot race. From our city of Pisa to the temple of Poseidon on the Isthmus of Corinth, we shall drive our swift steeds. A good half hour's start will I give to my daughter's suitor. But if I overtake him, my sharp spear shall pierce his heart and he shall die."

These were fearful words. The lightning speed of this King's horses was known to all. But the beauty of Hippodameia was like that of the new moon. Her suitors did not heed the King's warning. Prince after prince came to try his luck in the race.

Always it was the same story. Four splendid horses and a fine racing chariot would be brought from the royal stables. And the young prince would drive away.

Oenomaus stayed behind to sacrifice a fat ram to his protector, Zeus. Then, standing at the side of Myrtillus, his young charioteer, Oenomaus sped away after the bold young Prince.

The King's two famous mares, Psylla and Harpinna, were said to be daughters of the gods. Everyone knew they ran faster than the North Wind. Always, before the temple of Poseidon was reached, they overtook the four flying horses of the young Prince.

The sharp spear of Oenomaus then flew through the air to find the heart of the unlucky suitor of Hippodameia. And next day that poor young man's skull was seen on top of a pole beside the palace gate.

Twelve such gruesome skulls were there to give warning to the young Prince, Pelops. He looked long upon them. Then he turned back from that gate.

But Pelops had no thought to give up the race. Instead, he made his way with his charioteer down to the edge of the sea. And he called on Poseidon to come forth from his palace under the waves.

When Pelops had sacrificed a handsome black bull to honor the Sea God, there was a rumbling and roaring under the waters. The waves flew apart, and out from between them rolled a splendid gold chariot. Two magnificent sea horses pulled it, and dolphins with shining scales played along in the waters on either side.

In that magnificent chariot rode mighty Poseidon, his sea crown on his head, and his long beard blowing about his ruddy face in the breeze. His trident was raised high in salute to the young Prince who had called him forth from his palace.

"Mighty Poseidon, Ruler of the Sea! Shaker of the Earth! Father of Swift Horses! I come to you for aid." So Pelops cried out to the friendly god.

"Speak, son of Zeus," Poseidon replied. He was fond of this handsome youth. When Pelops was still a lad, the Sea God once had chosen him as his cupbearer upon Mount Olympus. Yes, he truly loved Pelops.

"Tomorrow I race with King Oenomaus, Poseidon," Pelops explained. "The prize is the hand of Hippodameia in marriage. That race I must win. But Zeus has given wings to the horses of this King. Only with your help can they be beaten. Lend me your aid, O Father of all Swift Horses."

"Zeus rides with Oenomaus, dear Pelops." The Sea God shook his head. "Zeus is far mightier than is Poseidon. There will be danger for you tomorrow."

"Always there is danger, O Lord of the Sea. I must die someday. It may well be tomorrow. Or it may be another day. Give me your help, I pray, that I may at least try to win my fair bride."

Poseidon struck the floor of his chariot with his trident.

Once again the waves parted, and four magnificent horses galloped out of the sea. Behind them they drew a racing chariot that shone like the sun.

"Test your driver's skill here, before you go to the King," Poseidon advised Pelops.

So the golden car, behind its four galloping steeds, rolled out over the land. So fast did it go that the charioteer's breath was forced out of his body. Pelops himself had to take up the reins to finish the run. Then like the wind, he drove off to the palace of King Oenomaus.

The King was surprised when he saw the shining gold chariot. "Surely," he thought, "those four noble steeds are the horses of Poseidon. This time I shall need Zeus by my side if I am to win."

"Hippodameia shall ride with you in the race, Pelops," Oenomaus declared. He hoped that having his Princess so close would take the young man's mind off his driving. But, of course, the cunning King did not speak of this aloud.

Pelops, too, knew that he must be clever. And he thought of a plan to make his victory sure. With Hippodameia walking beside him, he went to find Myrtillus, the King's own charioteer.

"Pull out the metal wheel-pins of your chariot, Myrtillus, and I will give you a rich reward," Pelops said to the young man. "Replace those metal wheel-pins with pins made of stiff wax, and no one will know. During the race, the heat made by the wheels' rolling will melt the wax. Then the King's chariot will have to stop."

[55]

At first Myrtillus would not agree to this plot. But Hippodameia added her pleading to that of Pelops. You see, at last she had fallen in love herself. To her this Prince Pelops was the husband she wanted to marry.

Myrtillus himself was young. Like almost every other man in Greece, he was under the spell of this Princess's beauty. He could not refuse her. That night wax pins were put into the place of the strong wheel-pins made of bronze.

Next morning the race began just as it had with the suitors whose skulls crowned the poles at the palace gates. With Hippodameia at his side, Pelops drove away from the city of Pisa.

Oenomaus quickly sacrificed the fat ram to Zeus. Then behind his two wingèd mares, Psylla and Harpinna, he galloped swiftly after them.

It must have taken some time for the stiff wax wheel-pins to melt. The King's chariot was pulling close to that of poor Pelops. Poseidon's temple, where the race was to end, was in sight not far ahead. Oenomaus was holding his spear ready to kill Pelops when he should pass him.

Just in time the wax melted. Without pins to hold them, the wheels of the King's chariot rolled off their axle. And in the great crash, King Oenomaus was dashed to the ground. As the Oracle had warned, the cruel father came to his death on the day when his daughter found her true love.

As the husband of Hippodameia, Pelops took over the throne of Oenomaus. Many other parts of Greece did he conquer. He ruled his broad lands well. Riches poured into his treasury. All over that part of the world Pelops was known as the "One blessed by the Gods." The great kingdom he founded was named Peloponnesus in his honor. Its people were the famed Peloponnesians.

It may have been Pelops himself who planned the very first games that honored Poseidon there on the Isthmus of Corinth. Surely he had reason to make such a festival for his protector. And surely these splendid Isthmian Games were a fit thanks offering for such a powerful god. In all that ancient world no other festivals were more magnificent, except perhaps the Olympic Games. But these Games, which honored Zeus, were not begun until many years later.

Who Put the Salt in the Sea?

*P*EOPLE HAVE BEEN WONDERING ABOUT THE SALT IN THE sea ever since the world began.

Some said the salt came at the time when the waters of the ocean were shut up inside the stomach of the giant frog in the moon. Storytellers in Africa declared that once God-who-made-the-world sent millions upon millions of mosquitoes to drink up the ocean. As in the fairy tale of the Moon Frog, this God was angry with the sea because it rolled too far over the land. It was when those millions upon millions of mosquitoes spat the ocean back into its bed that men first noticed its waters had a salty taste.

Still another answer to the question "Who put the salt in the sea?" is found in an old tale from countries in Northern Europe. The story was told in Denmark and

Sweden, in Norway and France. And it is about a magic stone mill which ground anything, yes, anything its owner desired.

In the tale there are giants and gods, kings and Viking warriors. There are two enormous slave girls who alone could turn the magic mill. And there is also just punishment for the selfishness of their greedy masters.

It all happened in the "Golden Age" of the North Countries, when the gods came down from their Heaven to rule on the earth. Frey, the God of Gladness, was then King of Sweden. His son, Frodi the Peaceful, was the ruler of Sweden's neighborland, Denmark.

O, that was a happy time, that Golden Age of the Northern Gods. It was a time without war. Countries were friendly then. And their kings often exchanged happy visits with one another.

The key to the magic in this tale of the salt in the sea was a huge stone mill. Its two massive stones had been a gift to King Frodi from a giant with the strange name of Hengi-Kiaptr, or Hanging Jaw.

The mill had a name too. In those days people gave names to things as well as to living creatures. Indeed, they spoke of their swords and their spears and their magic tools as if they lived and breathed and had minds of their own.

Everyone in those North Countries had heard of the spear, "Gungnir," which was made by the famous dwarf blacksmiths of the Gods. Gungnir, they said, never, never failed to find his mark.

Then there was the hammer of Thor, the fierce God of Thunder. "Miolnir," the Crusher, was that hammer's name. And no matter how far Miolnir might be thrown, he would fly straight back to his owner when his blow had been struck.

So no one thought it at all strange that the giant's mill in this tale should be called Grötti.

"Grötti will make good magic for you, Peaceful Frodi," Hengi-Kiaptr promised the King. "You have only to start the upper millstone to turning, and sing this song:

"*Grind! Grind! Grötti, grind*
What thy master hath in mind.

Speak your desire, Frodi, and whatever you name will come forth from between these magic millstones."

Who would not have been pleased with such a promise? King Frodi set the day for the first public turning of his magic mill. "On that day," he declared, "Grötti shall grind us gold and good fortune."

Flags flew. Trumpets were sounded. Crowds gathered in the courtyard of Frodi's great palace to see the wonder performed.

There were shouts, but shouts of disappointment when Frodi's slaves tried to turn the giant millstone around. For the stone did not move. One, two, three, four strong men joined in the task. Grötti did not budge.

The mightiest warriors in all Denmark then tried their strength. They had no better luck.

[63]

Oxen were harnessed to the millstone. Alas, it stood still. No man nor beast in all Frodi's kingdom was strong enough to start the mill, Grötti, to grinding.

It was during a visit to Sweden that King Frodi found the answer to his problem. While he was staying in the land of his father, King Frey, he noticed two giant slave girls. Enormous creatures they were, and their names were Menia and Fenia.

"What muscles those two have," Frodi said to Frey. "Surely the two of them could turn my millstone for me. Bring me their master so that I may buy them from him."

That's how it happened that Menia and Fenia found a new master and a new task to perform. King Frodi and his court shouted with joy when they easily started Grötti to grinding.

With a push and a pull of their strong arms, Menia and Fenia turned the magic millstone around and around. And as it moved, Frodi gave his first command:

> *"Grind! Grind! Grötti, grind*
> *What thy master hath in mind!*
> *Grind me gold!"*

The Danes watched with wonder as a stream of bright golden coins flowed forth from the mill. On, and on, and on came the coins until the royal treasury would hold no more.

> *"Grind! Grind! Grötti, grind*
> *What thy master hath in mind!*

[64]

*Grind me clothing and food
For all in this land."*

This was King Frodi's second command. And as the giant, Hengi-Kiaptr, had promised, there were fine clothing and good food for every family in Denmark.

One would have thought that King Frodi would have been content with this good fortune. Why did he command Grötti to grind more, and more, and more? O, it is too bad when good people become greedy.

Frodi gave no thought at all to the poor slaves, Menia and Fenia. Only for as long as a cuckoo called would he allow them to rest. Only for the time it took to sing one little verse of one little song, would he let them stop grinding.

Now, even giant creatures like Menia and Fenia grow weary of working.

"Master," they begged, "let us stop for a while. Our arms are sore. Our backs ache. We beg for a short rest."

But the greedy King only cried, "Grind on, slave girls! Grind on!"

Around and around the mill, Grötti, was turned. Menia and Fenia had no choice but to obey the King. For his warriors stood by, ready to punish them if they refused.

But when the night came, it was quite different.

"Our master and his warriors now sleep," Menia said to Fenia. "No one is here to tell us what we must grind. Let us now give the order. Let us think up a way to punish our selfish King."

Fenia lifted her hands from the millstone and replied, "Peace in this land is Frodi's great boast. Let us grind him a war. Mysinger, the Viking, and his ship filled with bold warriors sail the sea not far away. Mysinger would like nothing better than to land upon Denmark's rich shores. Grötti shall grind us a war between Mysinger and Frodi. And then we can escape."

Well, that's how it came about that, while the Danes slept, Mysinger landed with his fierce band of Vikings. At midnight they came to surprise Frodi the Peaceful. Silently they marched upon his royal palace. His guards were killed. Houses were burned. No longer were there peace and good fortune in Frodi's land.

The Viking victor carried off many of Frodi's rich treasures. And none did he take with greater joy than Grötti, the magic mill, and the two slave girls who could turn it.

All in the North Countries knew the story of Grötti. All had heard about the Grötti song which brought such good fortune.

The Danish shore was still in sight when Mysinger set Fenia and Menia to turning the magic mill on his Viking ship.

"What shall I command Grötti to grind first?" the Viking said to himself. He thought of all the cargoes he had ever brought back in his ship from foreign lands.

"It shall be salt. A cargo of salt!" he announced to his men. "Our ship filled with salt will make us all rich."

[66]

"Grind! Grind! Grötti, grind
What thy master hath in mind.
Grind me salt! Pure white salt!"

And to the slave girls, Menia and Fenia, he shouted:

"Turn! Turn! It is my will
That you should turn
This magic mill!"

A river of fine white salt began to flow from between Grötti's two millstones. Around and around the stone turned. And out flowed the salt. The ship soon was filled halfway up the mast.

"Your ship is full now, Master. May we not rest?" the slave girls begged Mysinger.

But if Menia and Fenia thought they now had a less selfish owner than King Frodi, they were mistaken. Mysinger, too, let his greed overcome him. His answer to their plea was only another shouted command:

"Turn! Turn! It is my will
That you should turn
This magic mill."

For not even so long as a cuckoo's call would the Viking allow the slaves to stop. And before he knew what was happening, the piles of salt rose to the top of his mast. They were so heavy, indeed, that his ship began to sink under their weight.

"Stop! Stop! Slave girls, stop!" the Viking screamed when he saw that his ship was going down.

But the slave girls kept turning and turning the magic millstone. And down, down under the waves went the proud Viking's ship.

Fishermen of the west coast of Norway still point to the place where the mill, Grötti, sank to the sea bottom. They show strangers a great whirlpool there in the ocean, with the water always swirling around and around.

The name of this whirlpool is the "Maelstrom." It comes from two words—"Malen," which means "turning," and "strom," which means "stream." The eye of this whirling water, so the legend goes, is just over the hole in Grötti's round stones.

Old people say that Menia and Fenia are down there, still turning the mill and grinding out salt. They insist that it was Grötti who first put the salt in the sea. And for people of olden times, who knew nothing of science, this was perhaps as good an answer to the question as any other.

Whistle the Wind

WHISTLE, MEN, WHISTLE!" THE CAPTAIN OF THE SMALL fishing boat called to his crew.

"Whistle the wind up out of his sleep. Asleep he must be. For not a breath of a breeze is he blowing against our boat's sails." The ruddy-faced fisherman of long ago shook his head as he looked across the still ocean. Like a sheet of smooth glass, it stretched out on all sides of his motionless boat.

"The waves do not move. Aye, the wind is asleep," one of the sailors agreed. He held out his hand, upon which lay a white feather from a sea gull's breast.

The other men, too, fixed their eyes on the bit of white down. They were hoping and hoping that when they whistled, a breeze would come and carry it off. But the feather just lay there on the man's palm. It was as still as their boat.

"We should have a 'wind cloth' such as my grandfather used to tell about," another one of the crew said. "He bought such a cloth that would bring the wind, from a witch up in Lapland. It was only a thin strip of cloth with three knots tied along it.

"For a fair breeze my grandfather untied the first knot. For a true wind, the second knot had to be undone. But he always took care not to loosen the third knot, lest a hurricane come and upset his boat."

"Did the wind cloth always bring the breeze?" the Captain asked.

"Well, that I don't remember. I guess it did, for my grandfather prized his wind cloth very greatly." But the sailor had to admit that he had not seen this wonder with his own eyes.

All day these fishermen of long-ago time had been talking of the wind they needed so badly. They were too far out at sea for their oars to take them far across the North Atlantic Ocean. Until the wind should fill their sails, they must wait there on the sea.

So they were passing the time, telling old tales. One man recited a riddle which his children had asked him the night before.

"What is it," he asked, "that runs without legs, that flies without wings, and screams without a mouth? It knocks at the door without any hand. You cannot see it or touch it, but you know it is there."

"The wind" was the answer, of course.

From time to time, the Captain of the fishing crew would repeat his order.

"Whistle, Men, whistle! Whistle the wind out of his bed!" Then he would add quickly, "But do not whistle too sharply lest he awake angry and blow us a gale."

Perhaps these sailors of long ago were too gentle in their whistling for a wind. For no breeze came. The sea gull's feather did not stir.

But they did not give up. They knew how it had been in the story of Saint Clement and the sea captain who rescued him from a rock in the midst of the ocean. They believed that, like that boat captain, in time they could actually whistle the wind into their sails.

This old tale has been told in many a fishing village. In France and in Scotland, in Sweden and in other northern lands it was believed by the men who took their boats to the fishing grounds off the island country of Newfoundland.

Long ago there was a time when no wind at all blew over the ocean. Day after day the sun shone, and the air was still.

"What has become of the wind?" fishermen asked one another. "How shall we reach the fishing grounds without wind for our sails?"

No one could answer the first question. Some said the wind was only taking a holiday. Others said it had gone to its home on the Island of Winds and would never come back. In all their minds there was the fear that the wind would not return in time for the new fishing season.

The King of France worried about his fishing fleet. And he sent forth his heralds to give his people this message:

"The King bids all seamen to try to bring back the wind to the ocean. To him who succeeds, the King will give the finest ship in all his royal fishing fleet."

Well, that would be a rich prize. And many a man tried his luck at raising a wind. Some tried by magic, perhaps even with "wind cloths" like the one used by the sailor's grandfather so long ago. Some said prayers to the saints. But no one brought forth even a gentle breeze.

The fishing season was well along. The distance to Newfoundland waters was great. Many a crew refused to set forth with only their oars to pull their boat over the sea.

But there was one French Captain whose name was Jean. He was liked by his men, and he persuaded them to put out with him from the fishing port of St. Malo.

It was when they had rowed far from the shore that they came upon the strange rock. It was a sharp jagged rock with broken edges that could easily wreck a boat. But the most curious thing was that the waves were rolling about it as if they were blown by a wind. How could this be when all other parts of the ocean were as still as glass.

For all there was no wind, the sea waves were dashing themselves against this rock. Their spray broke over its highest tip.

"Look, Captain Jean, look! There's a shipwrecked man on that rock." One of the crew had spied a dark figure clinging to its wet top.

In spite of the danger that his boat might be thrown by the waves upon the sharp crag, Captain Jean ordered his men to row alongside. And somehow or other they got the man safely off.

And there was another strange happening there at the rock. As soon as the shipwrecked man was safe in Captain Jean's boat, the waves stopped their rolling. The danger was gone. The sea was as calm there as everywhere else.

"Where do you go, Captain Jean?" It was strange that the shipwrecked man knew the name of the fisherman who had never seen him before.

"We are bound for the fishing grounds off Newfoundland," the good Captain replied. "But it will take us a long time without any wind."

"Do not make the trip now, my friend. Turn back to St. Malo and set me ashore." That was what the stranger demanded, to Jean's great surprise.

"I could not do that, for the fishing season is short." Captain Jean was almost angry. "I must bring back my boat full of fish or my family will starve. I have waited too long already for a wind to fill my boat's sails."

"All the same, my good Jean, you must change your plan. It is God's will that I go at once to St. Malo. In return I promise that your family shall not want. I will bring you far better luck than you would have on the fishing grounds."

So strong was the stranger's promise of good fortune that Jean turned his boat around. As fast as they could, his men rowed it back to the port of St. Malo.

As they watched the boat near the shore, the Captain and his strange passenger stood talking together.

"What would you like to have most in all the world, Captain Jean?"

"I want the wind back on the ocean." The fisherman did not have to think twice to find his answer. "I want, myself, to call the wind out of its hiding place. Then the King of France will give me the finest ship in his fleet for my own." Jean knew that he might as well wish for the moon, but that truly was what he wanted the most.

"You shall bring the wind back. You shall have your fine ship." Jean's eyes opened wide with wonder as the stranger went on. "I did not tell you before, but I am Saint Clement, who rules the wind and who cares for men on the sea. I put myself on the rock in your path to test your good heart. As reward for your kindness I will share with you my power over the wind.

"The wind has to obey my call. The Good God has willed it. The wind comes at my whistle. And it shall obey your whistle as well."

The good Saint placed his own lips upon the open mouth of the fisherman. He blew his own holy breath down the man's throat.

"Now, when you whistle, it will be my breath as well as your own which gives the call. You can bring forth the wind whenever you like. You shall whistle it out of its hiding place before the King's very eyes. And his ship will be yours."

And so it happened that, with the King and his court gathered on the seashore, Jean, the fisherman, set the wind to blow again over the waves. Whistling as the Saint taught him, he commanded the wind to fill the sails of all the ships in the King's fleet.

The sailors of St. Malo shouted, "Vive le Capitaine Jean!" which is to say, "Long live Captain Jean!" And they straightway set sail for the fishing grounds off Newfoundland.

From that day to this the wind has never been long gone from the ocean. The King of France kept his bargain too, and Jean got his fine fishing boat.

This fisherman's luck on the sea was as good as Saint Clement had promised. Indeed, he grew so rich that he really did not need to fish any more.

To show he was grateful, Captain Jean had made a splendid statue of the sailors' friend, good Saint Clement. In the name of all men who sail the sea, he set the statue up in his St. Malo church. There he could give thanks every Sunday to the Holy Man who had taught him to whistle the wind out of its hiding place in time of too great a calm.

This story explains how it is that, even today, Saint Clement receives the prayers of sailors. It tells why men like the Captain of the becalmed boat in the beginning of

this chapter kept calling upon his crew to whistle for the wind.

If you ask whether, at last, the wind really came in answer to their whistling, I could not tell you for sure. But let us believe that it did. Let us hope that before their lips were too tired to whistle again, the sea gull's little feather stirred in the sailor's hand. I myself feel sure that the wind came and blew it over the side of that boat into white-capped waves.

The Dancing Fires
of Saint Elmo

PULL IN THE NETS! MAKE FAST THE SAILS! SAINT ELMO comes to warn us. A great storm is near."

When they heard these words from their Captain, the sailors looked sharply up at the mast of their fishing boat. The afternoon sky over their heads was black with racing clouds. The sea had a cold, steely-gray color. But the warning signals they sought and found were the little tongues of blue flame dancing along their mast.

"Saint Elmo! Saint Elmo!" The cry rose from all the crew. The dancing fires of the good Saint had come once more in time to warn them of a storm.

Like tiny balls of fire, the blue lights rolled along the

mast and its crosspoles. They skipped from one part of the topsail to another. Some even ran down the ship's ropes and across its deck.

The Captain's boy cried out when one of the wee bits of fire rolled over his hand holding on to the side of the boat.

"But the fire does not burn!" he exclaimed in surprise. "I felt nothing at all when the flame went over my hand."

"To be sure." An old sailor nodded his head. "Saint Elmo's fire does no harm. It only shows us the good Saint is here to protect us in the storm."

By that time, all could hear the deep voice of the thunder, and not far away either. Across the dark sky ran long, forked flashes of lightning. The rain began to fall, and the waves rose. The little vessel was tossed about on the sea. It jumped like a porpoise from one wave to another.

"Saint Elmo, stay with us!" The sailors dropped to their knees as the storm broke in a fury over their boat. They raised their hands toward the mast, where the dancing blue fires were playing tag with one another. They could easily believe that the roar of the gale was the screaming of sea demons, riding on the wind.

"Saint Elmo, protect us!" they cried. So long as they could see the tiny blue flames they felt safe. Neither the wind nor the rain put the blue fires out. The waves which broke over the ship did not drive them away. No wonder the sailors believed their good Saint was keeping them safe.

For more than an hour, Saint Elmo's fires danced above the boat. Then the storm began to die down. The wind and the waves fell. Lightning no longer split open the clouds. And the bell of the thunder had ceased to toll its awesome song.

It was only then that the dancing fires flickered and went out. With their final weak flashes, the sailors gave a long whistle of farewell.

"Happy journey, Saint Elmo!" they cried, all together. "We thank you for bringing us safe through the storm."

One sailor declared he really had seen the good Saint himself in a bright flash of lightning. Another who climbed up the rigging to unfurl the sails said he had found up there on the mast a bit of the wax from the candles which the good Saint had used for his fires.

None of these seamen of so long ago doubted the legend that the dancing blue flames came from one of God's Saints. Seamen today see them still, for they really are tiny flashes of electricity which dance through the air before a thunderstorm.

People on land tell about them, too. How the tiny fires slide up and down a church steeple, or roll over a ridge of a barn roof. Pilots often see such tiny flashes of electricity on the wings of their airplanes before a storm breaks.

Writers of ancient times said that these dancing fires were stars. They said they were the stars into which the Greek Gods, Castor and Pollux, were turned after their deaths. And because they reminded many people of the tongues of Heavenly Fire in the Bible, others gave them the name "Espirito Santo" or "Holy Spirit."

But those who believe they are the fires of Saint Elmo tell the tale like this.

Long, long ago, a certain sea Captain was bringing his ship home after a journey. Like the Captain in the story of Saint Clement who whistled for the winds, this Captain was sailing off the shores of France.

Many things in the two stories seem the same. Each tells of a man in the sea who turns out to be a Saint. Each has in it a miracle by which the Saint rewards a stout-hearted Captain who saves his life.

"A boat! There ahead!" the lookout called to the Captain of the ship in this story of the dancing fires. "There's a boat without any mast. And the man in it has no oars."

No doubt the mast and the oars had been lost in the storm which had just swept the sea. The Captain's own ship had been tossed this way and that by the crashing waves. It did not surprise him to see such a small boat in trouble in such a sea.

"The man signals for help," the Captain called to his crew. "Make ready to take him aboard."

Safe and dry, well fed and rested, the rescued man was brought into the harbor. When the time came to say good-by, he thanked the good Captain.

"You saved my life, Friend. What shall I give to you in return?" he asked.

"I want no pay, Sir," the Captain replied. "It was only my duty to save you from the sea. I did it for the love of the Good God."

"Well, God will reward you, for it is one of His own Saints you have saved. I am Saint Elmo."

The Captain, at first, could not believe his ears. This man seemed to him a man just like himself.

"If you are truly a Saint," he said, "you must be able to make miracles happen. If you are truly one of God's Saints, make me a miracle."

Saint Elmo thought for a moment. Then he said to the doubting Captain, "What is it you fear most when you are out there on the sea?"

"It is a sudden storm I fear most," the Captain said quickly. "It is a gale that comes without warning and tears my sail into shreds before I can make it fast to the mast. It is the high, unforeseen waves that wash my men overboard. Yes, I fear a sudden storm most of all."

"Then no longer need you fear. No longer shall a storm come upon you without warning. I, Elmo, God's Saint, will see that you have time to make your boat ready for the wildest gale. I will light little fires which shall warn you when a storm is near. And may good luck follow your boat!"

When his holy passenger had gone, the Captain and his men talked among themselves of his strange promise. How could he warn them with fires far out on the sea?

They soon found the answer. On their very next journey,

they were sailing homeward in the dusk of a late afternoon. Suddenly tiny blue flames began to dance along their rigging. There was the roll of coming thunder, and the sky began to grow dark.

Like fluttering birds, the little flames ran along the mast. And the Captain remembered the words of Saint Elmo.

"The good Saint keeps his promise," he cried to his men.

"He has made for us a miracle. His dancing fires warn us of the storm, and we have time to make ready."

From that time on, sailors have looked for the fires of Saint Elmo. Some say that the name of this Saint was formerly Erasmus of Bible times. For in Italy, Erasmus was also called Elmo. Others think he may have been Saint Ermo, a Bishop from the island of Sicily. This Bishop was taken ill while on the sea, and he promised to give help in a storm, if the sailors would see him safely to land.

But however it was, these flickering flashes of electricity which fill the air before a thunderstorm, are today known far and wide as Saint Elmo's fire.

The Sea King and
the Fox

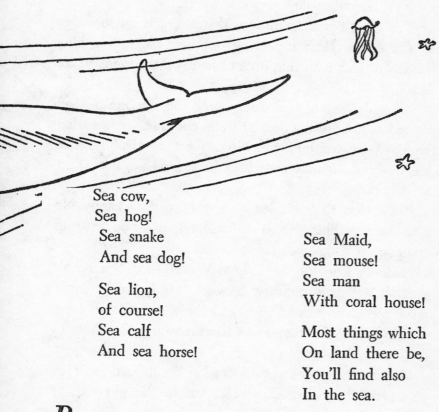

Sea cow,
Sea hog!
Sea snake
And sea dog!

Sea lion,
of course!
Sea calf
And sea horse!

Sea Maid,
Sea mouse!
Sea man
With coral house!

Most things which
On land there be,
You'll find also
In the sea.

*B*UT YOU WILL NOT FIND A FOX! AND HERE'S A STORY that expains why this should be so.

It was in the beginning of all things. God-who-made-the-world had placed on the land his men and his women, also the animals, both large and small. He had made birds for the air and fish for the sea. He was pleased when he looked at all the creatures gathered around him. He thought he had made a very fine world.

One day he was standing with his angels on the edge of the ocean. He was looking out over the rolling blue waves breaking with thin lines of foam on the sandy white beach.

Suddenly, out of the water, came the creature he had named as King of the Sea. The tale does not say just what kind of a sea monster it was. No doubt it was the biggest of all the fishes. It may even have been a whale, or a giant sea serpent.

It was clear that this Sea King was not at all happy. No smile stretched his great jaws. And straightway he began to complain to God-who-made-the-world.

"Mighty Lord of the Whole World"—the Sea King's tone showed how unhappy he was—"Lord, you have not given me for my kingdom any of these fine animals I see on the land. Why may I not have creatures like them in my watery realm?"

God-who-made-the-world looked at his animals gathered about him there on the seashore. And he thought perhaps he had been unfair to the King of the Sea.

"So it shall be!" he cried to the Sea King. "You shall have them." And he called his head angel to him.

"Throw into the ocean each kind of animal which you find on this beach." This was his command to the head angel.

The horse and the cow, the lion and the snake were straightway driven into the water. God even sent with them a man and a woman, who became a merman and a mermaid.

As each animal creature disappeared under the waves, a fox crouching nearby trembled with fear. "It will be my turn next, if I cannot think of a way to escape," he said to himself.

The angel had just thrown into the water a hog and a dog, when this sly fox came to him weeping. Tears ran out of the fox's small eyes. He made loud whining noises, so that the angel turned to look down at him.

"Why do you weep, Fox?" God's head angel asked him.

"I weep for my poor brother. O, that he should be the fox to be thrown into the sea," the fox sobbed.

"But I have not yet thrown a fox into the ocean," the angel objected. "I was just coming to get you."

"O, but you did," the fox lied. "It is that you do not remember, what with throwing so many animals into the sea. Look! You can still see my brother there in the ocean." And he bent far, far out over the clear water. Then he pointed to his own image, which looked up as if from a mirror.

The angel was puzzled. With his own eyes he saw the form and face of a fox which seemed to be already under the waves.

"Well," he said slowly, "I do not remember having thrown in a fox. Yet if one is already there, I do not need to send in another for the King of the Sea." And the angel made no objection when the clever fox ran away, far, far from the seashore.

The King of the Sea was happy when he called his new subjects about him. He looked them all over. He nodded with satisfaction when he saw the merman and the mermaid and the coral house they had found to live in. He was pleased with the sea cow and the sea horse, with the sea lion, the sea snake, and the little sea mouse.

"But I do not see here a fox," said the King of the Ocean. "How is it that the Lord of the World did not keep his promise to send me one of each animal that was there on the shore?"

One of the angels told how the fox had tricked them. And the Sea King straightway said, "That fox is clever. He is the smartest animal in the world. I would like to be as clever as he, and if I could but put his heart into my own body, perhaps I would be.

"Go to the land and fetch me that fox, that I may swallow his heart," the King commanded two porpoises. "And woe be to you if you come back without him."

"What if the fox will not leave the land?" The porpoises were not happy about their strange errand.

"Somehow or other you must persuade him. But bring the fox back you must." The Sea King truly thought that in the heart of the fox lay the secret of his clever tricks.

The porpoises found the crafty fox sniffing shells on the seashore.

"Are you the fox which outwitted the angel of God-who-made-the-world? Are you that very same one?" They wanted to be sure to make no mistake.

"I am that very fox. What do you want of me?"

"We come to salute you as our future king." The porpoises also had thought of a trick. "You have been chosen to rule after our present king in our undersea world. Our Sea King has fallen ill. He has not long to live, and he names you in his place."

"Why me?" The fox did not at first believe the porpoises' tale.

"Because you are the cleverest of all the creatures in the world, O, Fox." Well, of course this was true, the vain fox thought.

Now a fox likes to think he is important, just like anyone else. And the idea of being a king was pleasant. But still he was doubtful

"I am a land creature," he objected. "I shall drown in the ocean."

"No, sire, you shall not drown." The porpoises were delighted that the fox did not say "No" at once. "You shall ride high and dry on our backs over the waves. And once we have dropped you into the palace of the Sea King, you will be safe, for the water can be kept out. There you need have no fear of the fierce beasts of the land who now are your enemies. Think what a fine life you will have as King of the Sea."

So the porpoises persuaded the fox with fine promises.

And at last he climbed onto the back of the largest of them, and they set forth.

Soon, however, a great wave almost washed him from his slippery hold on the porpoise's back. Then he was sorry he had listened to these finny messengers from the Sea King. The more he thought of their promises, the more he suspected they had played him a trick.

"Tell me, Porpoise, tell me truly," he cried to the great fish on whose back he was riding, "am I truly to be King of the Sea? Or was it just a trick to get me into the power of your royal master?"

The porpoise felt sure that his prize could not escape now. So he shook with laughter. He laughed so hard that he almost jounced the poor fox off into the sea.

"To tell the truth, Fox," he said, between laughs, "it was a trick. Our master heard how you outwitted the angel of God-who-made-the-world. He thought it was clever. And he said, 'If I could just swallow the cunning heart of that fox, I'd be as clever as he.'

" 'Go back and bring me that fox that I may cut out his heart and put it in my own body.' That's what the Sea King said."

This was even worse than the fox had feared. He thought and he thought how he might yet escape.

"Alas, Porpoise," he said sadly. "You should have told me this before we left the land. I would then have brought my heart with me, instead of leaving it behind. The King will be very angry when he finds you have brought him a fox without his heart."

Now fishes are not noted for having quick wits. And the fox counted on this. Secretly he smiled when he saw that the porpoises took his words for true. They plainly were horrified.

"O, Fox," they cried, "did you really leave your heart behind you on the land?"

"Of course, Silly Ones." The fox spoke gaily now. "We foxes value our hearts. We never take them with us on a dangerous journey. We leave them in a secret, safe hiding place until we return.

"Take me back to the shore and there will be no reason for you to feel sad. I can get my heart for you in a flick of my tail."

The porpoises were doubtful. This sounded almost too easy.

"You had best do as I say, Friends," the sly fox continued. "If you do not take me to land, I shall tell the Sea King I offered to go back and get my heart for him. And that you would not let me. O, he will be angry then, not with me but with you."

The stupid fishes could think only of the punishment they would get from that angry Sea King. So they turned tail and headed back to the land.

"Hurry, Fox, hurry! Go fetch your heart!" they cried when they put their prisoner ashore.

With a leap and a bound, the fox galloped along the beach. Then he ran back for a moment to shout a laughing taunt at the fish.

"Stupid Ones, who ever heard of any creature walking around without a heart in his body? I had mine inside me all the time."

"Then you told a lie!" the porpoises cried.

"And why not?" the fox replied. "Did you not lie to me with your tale of becoming King of the Sea? Only my lie

was the best. And if I could fool God's own angel, why should I not get the better of poor fishes like you."

What happened to the unlucky messengers from the underwave world? I cannot say surely, for this was all so long ago. But the Sea King must have been angry. Big fish often eat smaller fish, as you well know. Perhaps the porpoises were served to the royal sea monster for his dinner that night.

You may believe this story or not, just as you like. But it is a true fact that to this day, although there is a sea horse and a sea cow, a sea snake and a sea lion, a sea dog and even a little sea mouse, no one has ever found a sea fox.

The Ice Ship in
the Hot Sea

THERE ARE MANY STRANGE THINGS ABOUT THIS WORLD we live in. And one of the strangest is the Northern Lights, whose other name is the "Aurora Borealis."

People who cross the far northern seas often see these beautiful curtains of light. Darting and flashing, their colors run over the night skies like giant fireworks. Sparkling white and dripping red! Blue and yellow! Green, orange, and rose! The rainbow-colored lights hang high above the northern ocean like necklaces of bright gems.

"Aurora Borealis" is the name that was given these flashing lights by the ancients. Aurora was Latin for "rosy dawn." And Boreas was the name of the wind from the north.

In many countries there are legends about how these strange lights first came into the sky. In Eskimo Land, where they so often are seen, children used to believe that

their dancing brightness was made by heavenly spirits at
play. In Japan, long ago, boys and girls were told a different
tale, the tale of the Ice Ship in the Hot Sea.

In the Japanese story another wonder of the world is
explained. This second wonder is the strange stream of
warm water that flows around and around in the cold
Pacific Ocean.

"Kuroshiwo" is the name the Japanese give this giant
warm river in the midst of the sea. In other lands, like our
own, it is known as the Japan Current.

The Japanese legend says it all happened when the world
was the home of the Gods as well as of men. One of the
most powerful of the Gods then was the Goddess of Fire.
She lived, it was said, in a mighty volcano, the biggest
volcano on all the Japanese islands. Who knows but that
it was the sacred mountain Fujiyama itself?

The red light of her fire could be seen far away. The
warmth of the red-hot rock lava which her volcano spit out
could be felt by ships on the sea.

Yes, the rosy light from the volcano of the Goddess of
Fire could be seen across the vast ocean, even as far away
as the North Pole. There, so the old story said, the Goddess
of Cold could see it from her icy throne on a glacier. Just as
a volcano seems a fitting home for a Goddess of Fire, so
a river of ice, a great creeping glacier, seems a good spot for
the home of the Goddess of Cold.

As you can understand, these two powerful goddesses

were jealous of one another. The Goddess of Cold, especially, envied her southern sister. In her far northern land, much of the year, the day was as dark as the night. And on such days the Cold Goddess hated to see the warm rosy light in the south given by the volcano of the Fire Goddess. She badly wanted to get some of this light for her land.

One dark winter day, the Cold Goddess called her oldest son to her side.

"My dear Son," she said to this Ice Prince, "the Goddess of Fire outdoes us with her brightness. We must get it away from her. We must take her a prisoner and force her to share this brightness with us. You shall go to the south and bring her back to our land."

"But how shall I travel so far over the ocean, my Mother?" The Ice Prince was a brave youth. He was handsome too. But he also was wise enough to know that his mother was sending him forth on no easy journey.

"We shall build a strong ship of ice. Ice rides well on the water. Your ice ship shall carry you and our army to the bright land of the Goddess of Fire."

Now, please do not ask how the giant ice ship was made. Nor what guns were used by the army from the northern Land of Cold.

Perhaps the ship was carved out of a glacier. Or perhaps it was only an enormous iceberg. I was not there, so I do not know. But the story says that the ship also had sails made of ice. And that the ice guns of the soldiers really could kill.

"Go with my blessing, my Son! Go, and do not return without the Goddess of Fire!" This was the parting command from his mother to the Ice Prince.

You can imagine the excitement in Japan when the giant ice ship was sighted.

"What shall we do?" the Fire Goddess said to her favorite daughter. "We have no weapons big enough to sink such an enormous ship. How shall we drive these strangers away from our shores?"

Now this Fire Princess was clever as well as beautiful. That is why her mother, the Goddess, often asked her for her advice.

"Our lookouts declare this giant ship is made of ice," the Fire Princess replied. "Fire melts ice. So why should you not send your fire out to melt the ice ship before it can land its soldiers on our island? Heat the ocean water with the hot lava from your volcano. Then the ice ship will disappear."

You can see by this just how clever this Fire Princess was. And you can be sure her mother followed her plan.

"Throw out your fire, my volcanoes!" cried the Fire Goddess. "Let your red-hot lava run quickly down into the ocean. Let it make the sea hot so that our land shall be saved."

At once all the volcanoes of Japan threw fire out of their mouths. Soon the ocean around the Japanese islands was boiling hot. Well, perhaps it did not actually boil. That was just the way the old storytellers had of saying that it was hot enought to melt an ice ship.

From the top of a volcano, the Fire Princess watched the giant ice ship grow smaller. She saw the hot ocean filled with drowning men from the northland.

Then, suddenly, her eyes fell upon the handsome son of the Cold Goddess. Even at such a distance she could see that he was the most handsome young man in the world. So fine a young Prince he was that her heart filled with love for him.

Down the sides of the fiery volcano she ran. Into the hot ocean she threw herself. And she was just in time to save him.

The Ice Prince was drowning, but she pushed a slab of cooled lava under his hands. The Prince took a firm hold and pulled himself up onto it. Strangely, it floated as well as a wooden raft. And he reached the shore safely.

No doubt you have already guessed that the handsome Ice Prince fell in love with the Fire Princess. Had she not saved his life? Had she not a bright, shining beauty such as he never before had seen in a girl's face? Was it strange that he should wish to make her his bride?

But the Fire Goddess would have none of this plan. She ordered the bold Prince to go back to his cold land. She did not foresee that he would take her dear daughter along with him.

How did the Ice Prince and the Fire Princess travel to the north without his ice ship? The story does not tell. Perhaps the sea gulls carried them there on their backs. Or perhaps they rode on a magic boat made out of lava.

All such things were possible when the Gods lived on the earth.

In any case, they came at last to the kingdom of the Goddess of Cold. But she had no welcome for either of them.

"You return without bringing the Goddess of Fire, as I commanded, my Son!" O, her greeting was angry. "This Fire Princess cannot take her place for my purpose. She does not have her mother's power to give fiery light to the world. She cannot make for us a volcano that will brighten our dark winter days. The light she sends forth is so pale that it shines only at night.

"You have lost our ice ship. Our army and our guns are at the bottom of the sea. I banish you from my kingdom." The heart of this Goddess was as cold as the ice of her glacier home.

So the two young people, the Ice Prince and the Fire Princess, went on and on to the north. They traveled until they were not very far from the North Pole.

It is from there, so this story says, that the Northern Lights come. They are made by the Fire Princess, who sends them forth as signals to her mother so far away. With her flashes of white, red, blue, and yellow, of green, orange, and rose, she is telling her mother that she is happy with her Ice Prince in the cold north.

Thus was the Aurora Borealis explained in ancient Japan. Thus it came about, so the old people said, that the warm ocean river, the Japan Current, flows through the cooler waters of the Pacific. Its water has been warm ever since the Fire Goddess heated it to melt that ice ship from the North.

The Ghost Ship

AHOY! AHOY! A SHIP AHEAD!"

The call came from the lookout in the round turret atop the mast. At his shout, the seamen below ran to the side of the ship and peered across the smooth water. At the line where the ocean seemed to meet the sky, they could see a tiny dark speck.

"There she is!"

"I see her, too!"

"She's dead ahead on our course!"

They all spoke at once. The appearance of a ship on the lonely ocean is an event for any crew.

"I don't like the look of her," the Captain said when they sailed closer. As he told it afterward, all the men on his boat saw the gray, three-masted sailing ship. She was lying low in the water as if she had a good cargo.

In the pink haze of the afternoon they could see her thin sails. And they were sure she was drifting. She lay still, dead ahead, as though she was awaiting them.

"When we were nearer we looked for her crew." This is the way that Captain told of his adventure. "Not one sailor did we see. There was only the ship's master, standing alone in her bow.

"Closer and closer we sailed. And this is the strangest thing of all. While we shouted 'Ahoy!' and 'Ahoy!' to the man, there in her bow, suddenly the ship was not there.

"It was then we guessed the truth." The Captain always shook his head at this point in his story. "It was the ghost ship of the 'Dutchman'! The ship people call *The Flying Dutchman*. We had had the bad luck to meet her there on the ocean.

"We all fell to our knees. We called on the Good Lord and his Saints to protect us. We prayed to Saint Clement. We begged Saint Elmo to watch over us. And the good Saints must have heard us. For we rode safely through the gale which blew in the wake of that ghost ship."

Sailors explain this gray ghostly vessel in different ways. Most of their stories agree that its home port was The Netherlands on the North Sea. Some say its Captain is a pirate who once made friends with the Devil. Others declare he is the ghost of a Dutch nobleman who murdered his brother and his brother's young bride six hundred years ago. His punishment for this deed is to wander forever alone in his ghost ship on the ocean.

Even more people like the story I have here for you. It tells how the wicked pride of a wealthy Dutch shipowner was justly punished. The Dutch Captain's name was Vander Decken, and it is thought that such a man really lived long ago.

Vander Decken's ship was the finest vessel that sailed out of the harbor of Amsterdam. In those olden times all the seamen of this great Netherlands port agreed that this was true.

They envied this sea Captain his handsome ship. It always was trim and so very well kept. Every sail was clean and whole. Every rope was like new. Every board in the ship's bottom was strong and firm. Its three masts were even covered with plates of iron so that no gale could snap them in two.

"I would not want to sail under Vander Decken. He is too hard a master." This is what some of the men said on the Amsterdam waterfront. "Everything on his ship has to be just so. Even the nail heads must shine!"

The sailors who then worked under the Dutchman would reply "Ya, Vander Decken is a hard master, it's true. But

Vander Decken pays us well. And he knows the sea and his ship. No one needs to be afraid in a storm with Vander Decken at the helm."

And the cargoes which Captain Vander Decken brought back from the East Indies! O, there were no other traders whose loads of spices and silks brought so much money.

It was no wonder that this Captain should have become rich. It was not strange that he should have been proud of his success. Nor that he should have boasted that there was no part of the ocean that he could not cross.

It was his pride and his boasting, however, that brought disaster upon him.

Vander Decken was sailing his ship home from the Indies. Loaded with treasures from the Orient, it was. And it was nearing the stormy southernmost point of the great continent of Africa.

The Cape of Good Hope! This is how we speak of this point of land today. But sailors also knew it as the "Cape of Storms." On all the wide ocean there was no place where the winds blew the waves higher, nor where more ships were wrecked.

Suddenly, that day, the sky darkened above the Dutchman's ship. The sea grew angry and gray. Its waves were swelling and swelling.

The wind was so strong that it blew the Dutch Captain's ship back on its course. And the sailors ran to the masts to make the sails tight. This was the only sensible thing to do in such a storm.

"Stop!" cried Vander Decken. "Stop! Let our sails fly. We shall go ahead and round the Cape."

"But this is a tempest," his men objected. "How can we sail into a hurricane wind? Let us turn about and ride with the storm."

While they spoke, the wind grew stronger. It whipped the waves higher. The sea broke over that ship with an angry roar and with masses of swirling white foam.

"Vander Decken fears no tempest, nor hurricane." The proud Dutchman was scornful. "No wind shall block Vander Decken's sails. We shall keep to our course. We shall sail round the Cape."

O, the man was daring! His men had to admit that. But they knew he was foolish, as well.

The Dutchman's ship was big. It sat low in the water with its heavy cargo. Yet the waves off that stormy Cape flung it this way and that, as if it were a toy.

Now the ship rose to the top of a mountain-high wave. Now it was flung down into the hollow trough between that wave and the next.

But that foolish Dutch Captain only laughed.

"Dog of a Sea!" he shouted. "Do you dare defy Vander Decken? Do you not know that no power on earth, nor in Heaven either, can take Vander Decken off his course?" And the Captain smoked his long pipe as calmly as if he were steering his vessel across a smooth summer sea.

"Master! Master!" The sailors were shocked. Now, indeed, they were afraid. "The sea demons will hear your words. Do not mock God in His Heaven, we beg you. Disaster is sure to come to us."

"I spit on the sea demons," the vain Captain screamed over the roar of the wind. "I care nothing for God in His Heaven. Not even God can keep Vander Decken from rounding the Cape this day." The man had surely gone mad.

The frightened sailors fell to their knees. They prayed God to forgive their foolish Captain. They called on Saint Elmo and other Saints, too. And suddenly, as if in answer to their prayers, there appeared on the ship's masts the blessed tongues of heavenly fire.

"Saint Elmo protects us!" the sailors shouted. "He sends his Holy Fires from Heaven to our masts as a sign."

But the foolish, proud Captain only grew purple with anger. He actually cursed God in His Heaven. And he fired the gun from his belt right at the Holy Fires. O, it was awesome to watch.

The storm then grew even fiercer. The wind blew up a hurricane. Waves rose one hundred feet into the air. And the Dutchman's ship was thrown from the crest of one wave to the other until it reached the dreadful ninth wave.

Then, all at once, there was silence on the sea. The scream of the wind was stilled. The boom of the waves ceased. And there came a voice out of the darkness.

Did that voice come from God in His Heaven? Or was it the cry of the sea demon who had been spit upon by the vain Captain?

[118]

Who knows?

But the words that were heard then on the Dutchman's ship were such as to bring terror even to the heart of this bold Captain.

"Vander Decken! Vander Decken! Poor, proud, foolish Vander Decken! You boast that no power can stop you from sailing the sea. Well, nothing shall stop you, not even your own wish. Sail the broad ocean you shall. On, and on, and on! You shall sail your ship on forever and ever.

"But no port shall receive you and your ship. No harbor shall offer its shelter to you. You do not fear storms. So the storms shall accompany you. Not shipwrecked yourself, yet shall you see the wrecking of many ships.

"Aye, Vander Decken, from this day no seaman will welcome the sight of you. As you have been envied and admired, now shall you be hated and feared.

"Alone you shall stand in the bow of your ship, with only the wind demons whistling in your sails for company. Your drink shall be bitter. Your food shall burn your tongue. Such sailing shall you have until the end of the world."

Does it seem strange that the storytellers of so long ago knew just what the fate of Vander Decken was to be? Well, no doubt the curse that was placed upon him and his ship did not take in his sailors. They had done no wrong. How they reached the shore, unless they swam to the Cape, no one knows. But it could only have been they who could tell just what took place. So they must have been saved from the curse of the Flying Dutchman.

The Flying Dutchman is known wherever men sail over the ocean. The story is told in this way, or in another way. But all agree that his ghost ship is still seen today, just as it has been for hundreds of years.

Kelea, the Surf Princess

*I*F A KING TELLS A STORY ABOUT HIS OWN COUNTRY, IT
ought to be true. So perhaps we may believe this one about
the lovely Hawaiian Princess whose name was Kelea. The
tale was often told by King Kalakua himself, who once
ruled the fair Islands of Hawaii.

Princess Kelea lived in even earlier times, when each
island had its own chief, or king. She was a sister, they say,
of Kawao, King of the important Island of Maui.

Like its sister islands, Maui lies like a green gem in the
midst of the sparkling blue waters of the Pacific Ocean.
Kelea loved her smiling homeland. She loved its high mountains. She loved its green valleys. She loved the low coastal
plain.

But more than all these, this Hawaiian Princess loved
the dancing waves that rolled up onto the shores of her

island. They were so blue under the sunny skies. And they broke into such splendid white surf.

"Kelea must have been born on the sea," said her brother, King Kawao. "Even when she was a baby, she was never so happy as when she was rolling about in the water."

In those times, boys and girls of these Islands learned to swim before they could walk. Most of their games took place in the shallow water along the beaches. They played hide-and-seek in the white surf. They played tag in the waves.

Early they learned to ride over the rolling waves on long boards sliced out of the trunk of the breadfruit tree. The surfboards of Hawaii were broad, and long enough for a tall man to lie down upon.

Fathers made smaller surfboards for their children to ride upon. But they were just like the ones the older surf riders used. Their sides were curved slightly. Their rounded ends let the water slip easily past.

It was fun to swim out with a surfboard, beyond the breaking waves. It was like flying to ride back to the beach on the long rollers.

No other girl, and no boy either, could swim better than Kelea. None on Maui Island could dive deeper into the warm, still waters of a lagoon. None could bring up more beautiful bits of coral rock from the sea bottom.

Kelea was sure, too, on her surfboard. No roller was too high for her to take. Somehow, she knew just how to keep ahead of a breaker which might dash her off into the sea.

That is why she was known far and wide as Kelea, the Surf Princess.

People on the shore often stopped to watch the small Surf Princess. "She is too daring," they often cried out. "She goes out when the waves are far too high. One day she will be drowned." But, luckily, that did not happen.

Time passed. The child Kelea grew up. At last she was of an age to be married, and many young men sought her as their bride. But she would have none of them.

"I will marry no man who cannot ride the waves better than I," she would say to each one. And then she would lead him down to the beach.

It was a fine sight to see the fair Princess on her surfboard. Her black hair streamed out behind her when she surfed to the shore. Her dark eyes shone as bright as the sun in the blue sky over her head.

In those days most surf riders lay flat on their boards. Or they knelt on one knee. Few could stay up on both feet so long as Kelea could.

"All Kelea wants for a husband is a surfboard," the disappointed young men declared when they failed to pass her test. For a long time none was able to outride this daring daughter of the sea.

Then came Lo-Lale, a handsome young prince from the Island of Oahu. The royal storyteller, King Kalakua, said he came in search of a bride because his people wished him to marry.

Lo-Lale had once before chosen a bride. The wedding

day had been set. But before the marriage feast could take place, his bride had been drowned. A sudden storm had overturned her surfboard in the sea.

Two years had gone by. Yet Lo-Lale had not sought for another bride.

"Lo-Lale, you must marry," his father said to the Prince. "You must have a wife to give you a son who will rule after you."

So Lo-Lale set forth to find a fair bride. Tales of the beauty and grace of the Princess Kelea were told then through all the Islands. And one day, in his canoe, Lo-Lale arrived on the Maui beach. He had come, himself, to see if the tales could be true.

There, in the sea, he found Kelea, swimming and surfing with her friends. Never had he seen a girl with so fair a face. Never had he known one who stood so sure and so free upon her surfboard.

In the bright sun, Kelea was like a figure of bright shining copper. Lo-Lale fell in love with her at very first sight.

"I will marry no man who cannot ride the waves better than I." Kelea spoke thus to Lo-Lale, just as she had to the others who came courting her.

Hearing these words, Prince Lo-Lale laughed. For he was the best surf rider of all the young men on the large Island of Oahu.

It was breath-taking to watch the two, Kelea and Lo-Lale, come to the shore on their surfboards. Side by side, they would swim out beyond the breakers. Like fish, they would dive through the highest waves. Then their dark heads would appear, out beyond the rollers, in the midst of the ocean.

Side by side they would ride a rolling wave in to the shore. Sometimes Kelea would beach her board first. Sometimes it was Lo-Lale. The Surf Princess had to admit that this young Prince was as daring and as sure as she was herself. And when it came to riding the rollers in a canoe, he was far better.

Lo-Lale was strong. He could manage a canoe that would need two ordinary paddlers to bring it safe through the surf. The people watching on the beach cheered when he took his canoe out upon the high waves.

One day her Prince invited Kelea to go out with him in the canoe. There were black clouds in the sky, and King Kawao begged his young sister not to go with Lo-Lale. Also, it was the month of the hurricanes.

But Kelea would not listen to his warning. She settled herself in the canoe, and Lo-Lale dipped his paddle into the sea.

Out, out, and out they went, far beyond the breakers. They were ready to turn about to ride the waves to the shore when the hurricane came.

The great winds drove the canoe out to sea. One gust turned the sturdy boat round and round. Another tossed it up into the air, as if it were a feather.

For once in her life, Kelea was afraid on the sea.

Lo-Lale's canoe stood first on one end, then on the other end. Often it seemed about to break into pieces.

"Do not be afraid, Kelea," Lo-Lale cried out above the noise of the wind. "Lie flat on the canoe's bottom. Then the waves cannot wash you out, and I will get you back safely."

It was splendid to watch Lo-Lale wield his paddle. How strong he was! And how fearless! Surely he would be a husband a Surf Princess could love and admire.

Well, the wedding took place. The royal capes of bright bird feathers, yellow and red, were put on the shoulders of the bride and the groom. Never on Maui had there been such a feast. A thousand pigs were roasted in the oven pits dug in the ground. A thousand coconuts were emptied of their sweet milk. A thousand different fish were eaten, and a thousand different fruits, too.

Flower-decked maidens danced on the beach. Their skirts of long, dry ti-leaves moved back and forth like palms in a wind. The air was filled with sweet music. Everyone sang and was glad.

But when the wedding was over, Lo-Lale said to his bride, "My dear one, I once lost a sweetheart in the sea. She was drowned in the surf. I cannot risk losing a wife, so I shall take you to the mountains on my Oahu Island. There we shall dwell, safe, far away from the ocean. Then I shall not always be thinking, 'What if Kelea should drown.'"

Kelea's heart was sad. To live where she could not swim

in her beloved sea! Never to feel the wind blow into her face as she sped over the waves on her surfboard! How could she bear it?

But a wife must obey her husband, even if she is a princess. Kelea tried to be happy in her mountain home. Her house was a palace, and one son, a second son, and a baby daughter were born to keep her from being lonely. You would think that she might have been content. But she was not.

"Are you still sad, Kelea?" Lo-Lale said to her one day. "Do you still long for the ocean?" The Prince truly was troubled that his dear wife smiled so seldom.

"I am like the small wavelet in the old story, Lo-Lale," Kelea replied. "Listen, and I will tell you how it was with that tiny wave.

"A man of the mountains one day went to the seashore. The blue waves were sparkling there in the sun. They were breaking into clouds of diamond-bright foam. The mountain man thought he never had seen so pretty a sight.

" 'I will just take one dancing wavelet back with me,' that man said to himself. 'It will be pretty to play with in my mountain home.'

"So he scooped up the tiny wave in a hollow piece of bamboo. And when he reached home, he poured it out into a coconut shell.

" 'But where is my wavelet?' the man cried as he looked down at the coconut shell.

"The water was there, to be sure. But it lay as still as

[129]

though it were dead. There was no wind to blow it into sparkling white foam. There were no other wavelets near to help it dance in the sun.

"'My pretty wavelet is sick,' that mountain man said. 'It does not dance any more, nor sparkle for me. It is dying with longing for its mother, the ocean. I must take it back to her.'

"Once more the man went down from the mountain. Once more he carried the wavelet in the hollow bamboo. And gently he poured it back into the sea.

"At once the wavelet was dancing and sparkling just as before. The man sighed. 'I was right,' he said, 'my wavelet was longing for its mother, the ocean.'"

Lo-Lale was ashamed when he heard Kelea's story. He had not meant to make his dear wife so sad. He had only wanted to keep her safe.

"But what good is it to be safe if one cannot be happy?" Lo-Lale shook his head. "We shall go back to the sea."

And he built a fine palace for her on the very edge of the ocean.

The light came again into Kelea's dark eyes. With her children she swam and she played in the sea. On her surf-board she rode once more over the rollers. The ocean winds blew her dark hair, and the salt spray kissed her cheeks. And she was as happy as happy could be.

The Crab That Tried to Swallow the Moon

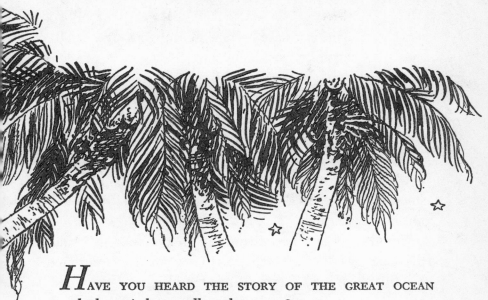

*H*AVE YOU HEARD THE STORY OF THE GREAT OCEAN crab that tried to swallow the moon?

It happened, they say, long, long ago in the Philippine Islands. It was in the cool of the evening. And a Filipino chief was giving a feast. All his tribe were there, the warriors and the fishermen and their women and children.

They were eating and eating. They were singing and dancing. And everybody was happy.

I do not know just how it happened. It was far too long ago. So I cannot tell you why the Chief's lovely daughter went away from the merrymaking. I cannot even tell you what her Filipino name was. But later on she was called, by the Spaniards who lived on the Islands, "Marina, Lady of the Boats."

Perhaps the Chief's daughter was tired of dancing. Perhaps the feast was too noisy. Or she may have eaten one mango too many and have become ill. But go away she did. And that was good, as you shall know.

There was a fresh breeze off the ocean that happy evening. The Chief's daughter found it pleasant to walk along the beach. The red sun had set. The waves were calm. The quiet was good after the noise of the merrymakers.

The Philippine Princess was moving slowly, looking nowhere in particular. Then suddenly she stopped. She stood very still, and she stared out at the ocean. She could not believe her eyes.

For there was a new island out in the sea. An island that had never been there before! How could such a thing be? But there it was, a small island, dark against the white foam of the waves that were breaking against it. The girl rubbed her eyes with her hand.

"That island was not there this morning," she said aloud. "Yet it is there now." Then she spoke again.

"The island moves. It is coming in toward the beach." And she was afraid.

Quickly the Chief's daughter stepped behind a huge coconut tree. So big was its trunk that she was well hidden. And from her hiding place there she could watch the strange floating island move to the shore.

"It is no island," she cried aloud. "It is a crab. A giant crab!"

Now she could see the monster. A crab it was, truly. But a creature so huge that it seemed to the girl ten water buffaloes could have stood on its back.

"The crab monster is hungry." She still spoke aloud, although there was no one but herself to hear. "It is seeking something to eat. Its claws are opening and shutting, and that is a sure sign."

Every Filipino knows the habits of crabs. This girl had played with the little beach crabs ever since she was small.

"Now the monster crab is making ready to spring. But what has it chosen to eat?" The Chief's daughter knew she was well hidden. She was sure that she was not to be the crab's prey.

Then she saw what it was. The giant crab was looking up at the moon in the sky. The moon's silver rim already showed above the tops of the trees. Yes, it was toward the moon that the monster crab was now waving its terrible claws. Its body was tipped back, and it stood so tall that it was higher than the waving leaves on the tops of the palm trees.

"The crab will swallow our moon. It will take the light from our sky. And what shall we do then?" The Chief's daughter thought that this giant crab really could reach up into the sky.

Around her neck, this young Princess always wore a horn made of a conch shell. Her father had given it to her. And he had said, "Blow loudly, my daughter, whenever you are in trouble. All on this island will know the sound of this horn. And they will come to bring help."

Now the girl lifted the conch horn to her lips. She blew a long blast. A second time she blew her call for help. Then a third time the cry of the conch-shell horn rang along the beach.

Only a small boy heard the first call. But at the second, the merrymakers stopped singing. They stood still in their dancing to listen and make sure. When the third call for help came, the musicians put down their drums and their flutes. The listeners dropped the food from their fingers. And everyone ran as fast as he could to help the Chief's daughter, who was in trouble.

"Quick, warriors! Quick! The crab will swallow our moon!" the Chief's daughter cried.

They were only just in time. The round moon was now well above the palm trees. The giant crab had grown so large that it truly reached up into the heavens. One claw was about to touch the round shining disk of the moon.

The warriors had brought their creeses along. Even such a great crab would feel the bite of the sharp curving blades of these famous Philippine swords.

The Chief's daughter herself led the warriors to battle against the monster from the sea. Somehow she, too, had gotten hold of a creese.

The crab heard the shrill cry of her tribe. And it turned its great body around.

With a swift blow of her creese, the Princess slashed through a giant claw. The warriors swung their creeses. They aimed at the other claws, but they all missed. They had to run fast to get out of the way of the angry crab.

When the Chief's daughter swung her sharp creese once

more, its point found the soft under part of the crab. So badly wounded was the creature that it now was no trouble for the warriors to finish it off.

The moon was safe! How the people all shouted! How they praised the brave Princess!

Sailors carved figures of the Chief's daughter from hard, shining wood form the Philippine forests. After that, no fishing boat sailed out of the island harbors without such a small wooden figure to bring it good luck.

Each moonlight night, the fishermen coming home bowed before the little statues of the brave girl.

"Thank you for light, Marina!" they said. "But for you, Our dear Lady of the Boats, our way over the water would be dark tonight. But for your bravery, the great crab that came out of the ocean would have succeeded in swallowing our moon."

The Friendly Sharks

IT HAPPENED HUNDREDS AND HUNDREDS OF YEARS AGO. It was when the Hawaiian Islands had fairy-tale kings. A king or a queen ruled each palm-fringed island. And another king or a queen ruled the ocean waters which washed each island's shores.

The kings and queens on the land, like the people they ruled, were brown-skinned South Sea Islanders. That is, their ancestors came from the beautiful green islands which dot the South Pacific Ocean.

Strange to say, the kings and the queens in the sea were all sharks. But they were not at all like the wild sharks which often opened their great jaws to swallow men.

Indeed, no! Sometimes these sea kings wore the shape of sharks. Other times they would change themselves into handsome men and fair women. And they lived in splendid sea palaces in caves under the Islands' beaches and cliffs.

More important than how they looked or how they lived, however, was the fact that these shark kings and queens were friendly to men. The ancient Hawaiians believed they were really the spirits of their own ancestors.

"Our guardian sharks warn us of coming storms," the Islanders said. "They send the bonito fish into our nets. When we are caught in a fog, they tell us how to steer our boats safely back to the shore. And when we ride the waves on our surfboards, they drive off the man-eaters that might attack us."

It was no wonder, then, that the Islanders worshipped these shark kings as their gods. Often they made for them the sacred drink from the awa root. They would pour this into the ocean, then ask the pleased sharks for their help. Some people today think that the Shark Gods were even more important to the ancient Hawaiians than the Gods of their volcanoes, who spat out fiery lava when they were angry.

Of all the Shark Gods of those times so long ago, none was more famed in the Islands than Ka-hu-pa-hu, the blond queen who ruled the ocean waters around the Island of Oahu. None was more powerful. And none took better care of the people whose island waters she guarded. When the Islanders swam in the sea, or rode on their surfboards, Ka-hu-pa-hu kept them safe.

"No man-eating shark shall ever swim here in our

waters!" This was the command that came out of her palace in the cliff. "Let one vicious shark come near Oahu, and he shall die. I, Ka-hu-pa-hu, have said it."

The man-eaters in the nearby waters feared the power of this Shark Queen. And they obeyed her command.

But now and again, a wild man-eating shark swam to Oahu from some other part of the ocean. Then there was trouble.

"The man-eaters from afar do not know of our law," Ka-hu-pa-hu one day said to her courtiers. "Who in this palace is bold enough to tell it to the sharks who swim in the faraway parts of the ocean?"

At first there was no answer to the Shark Queen's call for a messenger. Each shark in her palace well knew the dangers of carrying such a message to the man-eaters. Who among them would offer to undertake such a bold journey?

The silence was broken at last by brave words from a small shark. It was a very young shark, the son of the Head of Ka-hu-pa-hu's Palace Guard.

Ka-ehu-iki-mano-Puu-Loa! That was the name of that young shark. But no storyteller could ever use such a long name. In this tale it was shortened to Ka-ehu-iki, which means "small blond shark." The truth is he was named for the Blond Queen herself, and she was his godmother.

The Small Blond Shark was a favorite with all in that Queen's palace. The Queen herself smiled at her godson's courage, now.

"You are too young, dear Ka-ehu-iki. I cannot let you

undertake such a long and dangerous journey." The Shark Queen spoke firmly, but it was clear she was pleased.

"I am strong. I swim far. I have no fear of the man-eaters. And I would like to see the wide ocean." The young shark did not give up.

"You could not go alone, my Son. And who would go with you?" It was his father, the Head of the Palace Guard, who spoke now. He was afraid that his son, Ka-ehu-iki, was being too daring.

"I will gather companions as I swim from island to island. I will invite the bold King Sharks of Hilo and Kona, of Kohala and Kau to go along with me on my tour of the ocean."

Ever since he was born, Ka-ehu-iki had been different from the other young sharks. Before he had grown to a length of five feet, he could swim as far and as fast as his father and mother. Though he yet was so young, he had teeth four inches long and as sharp as a fish bone. One blow from his strong tail could knock away a much larger shark than himself.

"My blessing goes with you, then." Queen Ka-hu-pa-hu at last gave her consent. "Bring forth the magic oil, and cover the body of my brave messenger," she commanded her servants.

All watched in silence. The sacred oil was squeezed out of the awa root, out of the black coconut and the red fish. It was spread evenly over the hide of the young shark. Surely it would protect him.

"Say to all man-eaters that Queen Ka-hu-pa-hu wishes them no harm. But they must not swim within reach of her beloved island. This is our law." These were the words of his Queen which Ka-ehu-iki carried clear in his mind when he departed.

The young shark could not help showing off just a little when he swam out of the Queen's cave. He dived under the waves. He rolled and he turned somersaults in the sea. This was to be for him a magnificent and exciting adventure.

Ka-ehu-iki's first stop was at the Island of Hilo. One might think its two giant smoking volcanoes, Mauna Loa and Mauna Kea, would have frightened the young shark. But he showed no fear.

Nor was he turned back by the sharp words of the guard at the entrance to the undersea palace of Hilo's Shark King.

"I am a messenger from Oahu's Queen, Ka-hu-pa-hu, and I come to talk to your King," he announced.

Now a messenger from one ruler to another is not to be turned away. So Ka-ehu-iki was taken before the Lord of Hilo's waters.

"I come to admire your fair island, O King," he said politely, "And I bring a message to any man-eating sharks who may swim off its shores." And he told the Hilo King Shark of the journey he meant to make across the wide ocean.

"Will you not swim the sea with me, O King of the Island of Hilo? It will be a fine journey and we shall see all the world. Perhaps we shall even go as far as the Island of Tahiti."

The young shark's friendly manner made his invitation attractive. The Hilo King was pleased with him. And after they had talked more of the wonders they might find in the ocean, he decided to accept.

This was the way it was also with the kings of the other islands. One by one they were won over by Ka-ehu-iki's joy in his adventure. It must have been a fine sight to see the line of kingly sharks swimming in the ocean behind the young blond shark from Oahu.

Only when they came to the narrow water passage between Maui and its island neighbors was there much trouble. These waters were the realm of a fierce war-loving Shark King called Kau-hu-hu.

Try as he might, with soft words and politeness, Ka-ehu-iki was unable to melt Kau-hu-hu's unfriendly heart.

"No strangers shall pass through my narrow waters. Not friend nor foe. Not even kings from Hilo, nor Kona, nor Kau, nor Kohala, and certainly not a mere messenger from Oahu." These were the words with which that Shark King barred their way out into the broad Pacific Ocean.

"We must turn back, Ka-ehu-iki." The other sharks were afraid. But their young leader only laughed.

"Perhaps this old King Shark is not so strong as I am," he cried. "Perhaps no one has put over him the magic oil made of the awa root, the black coconut, and the red fish. I do not fear him."

And to the wonder of his royal companions, the bold young shark called the war-loving King out to battle with him.

Kau-hu-hu took one look at the small young shark from Oahu. And he thought, "It will take only one good bite to finish off this foolish youngster."

The great jaws of the King Shark of Maui opened wide. But before he could snap them shut, Ka-ehu-iki swam right down his huge throat, and into his stomach.

With his sharp, pointed teeth, the young shark began to gnaw his way out again. From one end of the Shark King's body to the other, he chewed a passage that brought him safely out into the ocean at the monster's tail. Of course the Shark King was dead by then, and his great body floated away on the waves.

News of this victory came to the Great God of all the Ocean. He had been very angry with the war-loving King Shark of Maui, and he was pleased with Ka-ehu-iki. He called the young victor to him.

They were a strange pair, the ancient ocean Shark God with shells and sea moss upon his tough hide, and the sleek young adventurer whose skin still shone with the magic oil.

"You fought wisely and well, Ka-ehu-iki," the Ocean God said. "You shall win other victories as you swim on your journey. I shall give you a shark's strength second to none. And I shall give you also the power to put on whatever body you may choose for yourself, be it beast, bird, or man."

There was a fine feast for the young shark and his companions before they set forth again. Everyone praised him. It was a wonder he did not forget that he was only a messenger from the Queen Shark of Oahu.

But Ka-ehu-iki remembered. Everywhere he went he sought out the man-eating sharks and told them of her law. Now and then there was a fight, but the blessing of the Ocean God gave him the victory each time.

From Pacific island to Pacific island, even to far off Tahiti, the party of sharks from Hawaii swam safely. And safely they returned at last to their home waters.

It was when they came near Oahu once more that their strangest adventure took place. Just off a coral reef they met a fierce man-eating shark. They could tell by the way his small eyes searched the ocean that he was hunting for men.

"Who are you? And what are you looking for?" Ka-ehu-iki demanded of the strange shark.

"I am Pehu, and I am hungry. One of those surf riders will make me a good meal." Either this man-eater had not heard of Queen Ka-hu-pa-hu's law, or he was foolish enough to think he need not obey it.

Ka-ehu-iki was not, at first, sure what he should do. The man-eater was big, bigger by far than this young shark or his companions. The only way would be to think of a trick that would keep him away from the happy Islanders out riding upon their surfboards.

"Let us all swim to the shore together." Ka-ehu-iki pretended to be friendly. "We will attack the riders at once, and you shall have a good meal."

At the same time, he called his companions to one side.

"We must surround this man-eater. We must crowd him up onto the sharp coral reef. We must keep him there out of the water until he is dead." This was the plot of the small blond shark.

The rollers were strong and the surfboards moved fast. A great swell was coming when Ka-ehu-iki cried, "Now, Pehu, is the time!"

But to Pehu's surprise, the young shark and the king sharks swam close around him. They pushed and they shoved against his great body until they drove him toward the reef.

So hard did the hungry man-eater try to get ahead of them that he did not see where he was going. With a mighty dive he landed head first in a wide crack in the coral rock. He was wedged between the coral walls of the crevice. And though his monster tail thrashed about in the air, he could not get his head loose.

All the surf riders came to see the huge shark upside down in the coral. When his body was cut open, the hair and the bones and the teeth of men were found in it. O, the Islanders were angry then. They set fire to the dead shark and burned his body to ashes. People remembered how it was, because that part of their shore was given a Hawaiian name which meant "Here Pehu was burned."

A fine celebration was held in honor of Ka-ehu-iki. There were soft coconuts to eat and awa to drink. The hula was danced and many songs told of the small blond shark's bravery.

Queen Ka-hu-pa-hu herself hung a wreath of sea flowers about the young hero's neck. For that occasion, she and her courtiers and Ka-ehu-iki himself changed themselves into men and women. And their feasting lasted for a whole year.

When his father died, this young shark was given his position of honor as Head of the Palace Guard. And who better deserved it?

The Old Woman Swims the Sea

*T*HIS STORY COMES FROM THE ICY NORTHERN SEA. IT IS about the cold homeland of the short, sturdy people called Lapps.

With their reindeer and their fishing, the Lapps are happy in their tents along the shores of Northland. They are sorry only that their country is no longer as big as it was in olden times.

In the long, long ago, the Lapps were alone in this northern part of Europe. Their only living neighbors were the wild reindeer. And these were so many that no Lapp hunter wanted for meat or for good skins to make a tent for his family.

Indeed, at first the Lapps did not know there were any other people in all the world. For that was before men from Norway and Sweden and Finland came to visit them from the south.

The Russians, who lived to the east, were among the first of such strangers to discover the land of the Lapps. They came over the snow and the ice on their snowshoes and sleds. In the summertime they arrived also in boats.

"To get away from the Russians, our forefathers dug deep holes in the earth." The old people shook their heads at the thought of how hard life was then. "Instead of using tents that these strangers could easily see, people often lived for days in these underground pits. Like the fairy people, the Uldas, they had to hide under the rocks."

It is easy to understand, then, why the Lapps did not like those Russian raiders. There were battles between them. Sometimes it was the Lapps who were killed. Sometimes it was the Russians. But always more Russians came. They came and they came until they were tricked by an old woman who lived on a high ridge overlooking the sea.

Always, in those times, the Lapps were trying to think of ways to rid themselves of the Russian raiders.

But the best way of all was that of the clever old woman who lived on the shore of that northern sea.

"The Russians are coming. They are headed here for your ridge." The Lapp lookouts sent this warning to that old woman one day. "All the families have gone to hide in the pits. You must come with them."

"No," said the old woman, "I shall not hide. I am old, but I can take care of myself." O, she was a brave granny.

She did hide her silver treasures under the rocks, however. She was too old to run after the reindeer, so she had no herd to take to the back country where the Russians would not find it. Alone in her tent on the high rocky ridge, she was waiting when they came.

How could she have been so brave? Well, it may be she was part Ulda and had their fairy magic. Or it may be she was just wiser than they. Whatever it was, she turned out to be more than a match for that band of Russians.

"Granny," the raiders said when they came upon her, "Granny, you need not be afraid. We will not harm you if you will give us help. We will not look for your furs nor your treasures of silver, if you only will show us where the People of this land are hiding."

The "People" is what the Lapps called themselves. This came from the time when they thought they were the only people in all the world.

It was not so much the People that the Russians wanted to find. The old woman knew this. It was their reindeer and their furs and their silver treasure which they had taken away with them. The strangers were sure that if they could find the Lapps themselves, these would be close by.

"The People are not so very far away," the old Lapp woman said. "They heard of your coming, and they hid themselves on an island out in the ocean. They went off without me. And that was not kind of them."

The old woman, of course, was only pretending to be angry with her Lapp neighbors. She thought this would make the Russian raiders believe she would help them. And this was part of her plan.

"Take me along with you, Friends," she begged. "Give me some food, for I am hungry. Then I will show you the way to the island where the People are."

The Russians looked at one another. This was an easy victory. But surely an old woman like this one could do them no harm. She would make a good guide.

"When shall we start for the island where the People are, Granny?" They felt sure she spoke the truth.

"We must wait till the dark comes. We must not try to land until the People are all asleep. The People are clever. They are strong, too. If you come upon them in the day, they will see you and run. They will swim across the big water. You never would catch them."

"The old woman is wise. We will wait for the night," the Russians decided.

"And we cannot take the boats," the Lapp woman declared. "The lookouts would hear them when we landed on the shore. We shall have to swim." This, too, was part of the plot she had made.

While they waited for darkness, the old woman took her swimming jacket of birch bark from under a rock. I have said she was clever. And when you hear about her swimming coat, you will know I spoke truly.

The coat was made of thinnest birch bark, and inside it were many tiny seal bladder balloons. There was air inside these balloons, and with them to hold her up the old woman could keep afloat in the ocean for a long time.

In those times only the Lapps knew about swimming jackets, perhaps. At least none of the Russians who sat in her tent guessed what her shabby bark coat was for.

"We shall have to cross the small water to get to the island where the People are. We shall have to pass other islands. But we can easily find them, if you can swim?" The old woman looked at the Russians as she asked the question.

"O, we can swim easily if we have only to cross the small water," they replied. "But what about you, Granny? Can you swim that far?"

"I can swim a little. I can swim far enough to show you the way to the island where the People are." You see, she truly was clever. "Soon it will be dark. Then we can start."

With the coming of night, the North Wind began to blow, just as the old woman had known that it would. When it was dark enough she tied on her swimming jacket. She put on her fur hood. And she said to the Russians, "It is the time. The People now are surely asleep. They will not hear us coming in this howling wind."

"We shall need a light in the darkness," the old woman added. "I will make us a torch of this bundle of birch wood. I will hold it high. You can follow its light."

She was the first to jump into the sea. The Russians dived after her. Brr, it was cold. But the old woman did not seem to mind, and so the Russian men were ashamed to complain.

The raiders had no trouble in following their guide. Somehow, the old woman managed to swim in the sea, yet keep her torch dry.

They swam to one island.

"This is not the place," the old woman called back to her followers.

They swam to another island, and she said, "This is not the place either." Then they swam to a third island.

"The People are hiding on the fourth island," she told the Russians. "That one is a little farther out in the sea. I shall need to light a bigger bundle of birch sticks to show you the way. I do not swim so fast as you men, and you will quickly overtake me. So I will start first. Wait for a little before you come after me, so that I can stay ahead."

She told them that she would hold the torch steady. They could follow its light.

The old woman then jumped again into the sea. As she swam off, the Russians could see her bundle of burning sticks. Their fire was bright in the darkness.

But when she was just a short distance from shore, the old woman took out from under her jacket a flat piece of wet wood. Down on the water it floated like a wee raft. And she set her torch of burning birch sticks upright upon it. The sticks fitted into holes she had made. And the flame was well up above the wet wood.

The old woman laughed when she gave the tiny raft a push out toward the ocean. She smiled when she watched the wind blow her torch onward. Then she took off her fur hood and sent it floating after the torch. As she had planned, it too was carried out on the sea.

By a roundabout way in the darkness, the old woman swam back to the island she had just left. Soon she was in a safe hiding place among its rocks.

Meanwhile the Russians had begun their swim after her. Through the dark in the distance, they could clearly see the light of her torch. And they swam where it led them.

The North Wind was blowing. It sent the old woman's tiny lighted raft bobbing over the waves. Always, always, its light was ahead of the Russians swimming in the icy ocean. Then, all at once, the light was gone. No doubt a tiny wave had snuffed it out.

"Where is the old woman? Where can her torch be?" The Russians were worried. They called her and called her.

"Here is the old woman's fur hood!" one shouted to the others.

"She must be close by, then," said another. "We must find her if we are to come to the island where the People are."

"We must find that island if we are not to be drowned here in the sea." A third was growing tired with swimming and swimming in the cold ocean.

That third one was right. The raiders were then far out in the sea. The light they were following had gone out. In the black darkness they swam this way and that way. But they did not find the old woman. Nor did they reach an island's shore. Those Russians were lost. They never came back to the land of the Lapps.

And how glad the People of the north country were! The old woman was given the best of the meat whenever a reindeer was butchered. The men made her a fine new deerskin tent. For no one in that part of the north ever forgot the clever trick she had played to get rid of the Russians.

The hill where that old woman lived was renamed "Raiders' Ridge." Even today her story is told when someone asks how the ridge by the sea got its name.

The Whale That Smoked
a Pipe

KIT-POO, THE MICMAC INDIAN BOY, SAT IN THE BOW OF his grandfather's dugout canoe. The summer sun shone on the blue waters there, off the shore of that part of America now known as New England. A breeze blew through the black hair of the kneeling Indian boy. Like the men in that dugout, Kit-Poo was dipping a paddle in and out of the ocean.

The air was clear. Kit-Poo could see far, far across the water. His keen eyes were always looking for another boat. Sometimes he spied, in the distance, porpoises jumping in and out of the waves. Or nearer, a school of flying fish which had come in close to the shore.

Suddenly, the Micmac boy gave a cry.

"A whale! A whale! There, Grandfather, ahead of us. I see a whale."

The old Indian shaded his eyes with his tawny hand.

The others in that dugout, too, peered across the blue water. They were too far away to see the whale itself. But they quickly spotted the tall jet of white water which the creature was spouting up into the air.

"He blows a mighty puff of smoke from his pipe, Kit-Poo," the boy's grandfather said. And Kit-Poo's face broke into a smile at the thought of a whale smoking a pipe.

But the spout from the whale's head truly did look like a plume of white smoke. It reminded the boy of smoke which rose straight up into the air from his grandfather's pipe when there was no breeze to blow it to one side or the other.

"Did I ever tell you the tale of the whale that did smoke a pipe, Noojech?*" The old Indian smiled as he looked down at Kit-Poo.

"A whale that smoked a pipe! Where would a whale get a pipe? How could a whale light a pipe? And who taught him how to smoke it?"

"It was in the long-ago time," the boy's grandfather replied. "Anything could happen in those days of Glooskap and his magic. It was Glooskap, the Great Spirit, who gave that whale his pipe.

"Glooskap made the world and the people upon it. Glooskap made the animals for men to hunt, and the fishes for men to catch. He showed men how to carve their pipes out of stone. Why should he not also teach a whale how to smoke?"

*Grandson

"Well, why not, indeed?" Kit-Poo said to himself.

This Micmac boy knew all about Glooskap, the Great One. He knew that the magic of Glooskap was greater than that of all the giants and demons, of all the witches and wizards of that ancient time.

Glooskap was as tall as the tallest pine tree, so Kit-Poo's people said. Sometimes, when he stretched his arms into the sky, he could touch the stars. And like the boy's old grandfather, Glooskap liked to smoke his pipe of tobacco.

Tales about Glooskap's smoking were many. It was said he could fill his great pipe with all the tobacco grown in one year in all the world. And with one mighty draw on the stem of that pipe, he could turn the lighted tobacco to ashes.

Now, in those ancient days, there were those who were jealous of Glooskap and his magic. And none was more jealous than a certain proud wizard whose name was Win-Pe. At least that is how Kit-Poo's grandfather told the story that day in his dugout canoe.

Glooskap lived on an island far out in the ocean, he said. He had no wife, so an old woman kept house for him and his son, whom he loved dearly. She cooked their food well, and she mended their deerskin clothes. And Glooskap was contented there on his island. Whenever he wanted to go to the mainland, there was always his canoe waiting for him on the shore.

The only thing that annoyed him was this wizard, Win-Pe. Glooskap, who knew all things, knew this wizard was jealous. He was sure the man was only waiting a chance to do him a bad turn.

For days there had been a partridge running in and out of the bushes near the wigwam of the Great One. In those times men were as animals and animals were as men, and often those who knew magic could change from one to the other. If Glooskap had thought much about it, he soon would have found out that the partridge was Win-Pe, spying upon him. But he paid no attention.

The wizard's spying at last brought its reward. One day, he saw Glooskap put his canoe out from the island and paddle off for the mainland.

"Here is my chance! And this is my plan!" The wizard spoke aloud as he went over the plot he had made to hurt Glooskap.

"I will take away Glooskap's housekeeper and his dear son. And I'll hide the two of them deep, deep inside a cave where they cannot be seen.

"When Glooskap finds they are gone, he'll go out to look for them. And while he is searching the island, I'll steal his canoe. Then the Great One will have no way to get to the mainland. He'll have to stay here all alone. Who can say then that his magic is greater than mine?"

This was the plot. And at first it almost seemed as if it would succeed. Glooskap returned, and as soon as he beached his canoe, he went to his wigwam to find his housekeeper and his dear son. But when he lifted the bark-door curtain, he saw the wigwam was empty.

Straightway the Great One began his search of the island, just as Win-Pe had guessed that he would. He looked and looked for his housekeeper and his son. When he came back toward the landing place, he was just in time to see Win-Pe, the wizard, leaving the shore in his own canoe.

The thief was paddling hard, and in the boat with him were Glooskap's old housekeeper and his dear son. The Great One could see that they were tied up with deerskin thongs, and that they could not get themselves free.

How could Glooskap go after them without any boat? It is true he was taller than the tallest pine tree. But even his legs were not long enough to permit him to walk upon the sea bottom.

"I shall call on the whales to carry me to the mainland to rescue my dear son and the old woman," Glooskap said to himself. And with his great voice he sang his magic song which always brought the giant creatures out of the waves to his side.

The first whale that answered his call was a small one. The moment the huge foot of Glooskap set its weight on that whale's back, it sank down, down, far down under the waters.

The second, the third, and the fourth whale that came to him were not big enough either. But the fifth whale was the very largest whale in the ocean. It was quite strong enough to carry the Great Glooskap over the waves.

Astride the whale's back, Glooskap set forth. It was a

fine smooth ride at first. Then the whale began to stop swimming. Ahead he would go. Then he would just float. The trouble was that he was afraid he was coming near the land. The one thing the whale feared was that he should find himself out of the water. How should an ocean creature like him live high and dry on the land?

"Is the shore in sight, Great One? I cannot swim in low water," the whale said to Glooskap.

Remember, men were as animals then, and animals were as men, and they could talk to one another.

"No shore is in sight," Glooskap replied. He did not look very hard, for he did not want to have to wade through the low water to land.

"Is there not a dark line of shore ahead, Master?" For all they were so little, the eyes in the great head of the whale could see far.

"No, there is no shore at all." This was not really true, but Glooskap never minded about the truth when he wanted to play a trick. Kit-Poo had heard many tales of the pranks which the Great One had thought of to tease his brothers, the animals.

Then the whale thought it saw a shell under the waves.

"Do I not see a shell on the ocean's bottom, Master Glooskap? Do I not hear the voices of the clams?"

In those strange times the clams often sang. The big clams sang with deep tones. The small clams had high voices. Their songs could be heard easily by those who were riding the waves above their sandy beds.

"Well, I do hear the clams singing," Glooskap admitted.

"Tell me what the clams say, Master. I do not understand the speech of the clams."

"They say you can safely swim in the water here, Whale."

This was not really true either. For some reason, those clams did not feel friendly toward Glooskap. And the song they were singing was something like this:

> *"Dive under the waves, Whale,*
> *Into the sea!*
> *Drown Master Glooskap,*
> *He's our enemy."*

But since that whale did not understand the song of the clams, Glooskap was safe. And again he tricked the whale, singing a small song himself.

> *"The clams sing 'Hurry, Whale!*
> *Hurry along!*
> *Hurry! Swim swiftly!*
> *That's the clams' song.'"*

The whale still believed Glooskap. Like an Indian's swift arrow, the creature sped through the sea. Before it could stop, it had dashed itself out of the waves and up onto the beach. There it found itself high and dry, and quite out of the water. The more the whale struggled, the deeper it dug itself into the sand.

Glooskap was happy to have reached land without having

[169]

to wade through the water. He was grateful to the good whale which had brought him over the ocean on his search for his old housekeeper and his dear son.

But the whale was far from happy. Over and over it sang this sad song:

> *"Woe! Woe! Woe is me!*
> *I cannot live upon this shore.*
> *How shall I get back to the sea*
> *And in my ocean swim once more?"*

Now, Glooskap had really a very kind heart. The tricks he played on the animals were not meant to hurt. So, quickly to comfort the poor panting whale, he sang this answering song:

> *"No! No! It is not so.*
> *You will not die here on the shore.*
> *Into the water you shall go*
> *And in your ocean swim once more."*

It was not a very good song that Glooskap sang, but it did comfort the whale. And then the Great One took up the magic bow of bent maple wood which he always carried with him. With its tip Glooskap gave the whale's head a push.

Like an otter coasting down the slippery mud bank of a woodland stream, the whale slid over the sand into the water. Its great tail churned the waves in its joy to be in the ocean once again.

Turning, the whale swam back, to give thanks to Glooskap and to say good-by. The Great One had already lighted his pipe and was sending white smoke out upon the still air.

"You shall be rewarded for your service to me," Glooskap told the whale. "What shall I give you?"

And the whale, watching the contented smile on the face of the Master as he smoked his pipe, said, "O, Glooskap, I'd like to smoke a pipe just like yours."

"A pipe you shall have, Whale. And that pipe you shall smoke." Glooskap, from somewhere, brought forth a stone pipe. He filled it with tobacco and he set the tobacco on fire.

When he showed the whale how, the creature easily breathed the smoke in and out. At least, Kit-Poo's grandfather said that it did.

The Micmac boy thought he would like to have seen that whale swimming over the ocean, with its head out of water, smoking its pipe. He looked again at the live whale off in the distance, blowing its white spray into the air. And he could easily imagine that it, like the whale in his grandfather's story, was smoking a pipe.

The Little King on
the Viking Ship

*H*ERE COMES THE *skald! * THE *skald* IS AT OUR DOOR!"

This glad shout was often heard in the manor houses of North Europe in times long ago. In Norway, in Sweden, and in their small neighborland, Denmark, *skald* was the name for a poet who made up songs about great men and their noble deeds.

All in the manor house would hurry to welcome this traveling teller of tales and singer of songs. A place for the *skald* was quickly set on the supper table. A bed was made ready so that he would not hurry away. A comfortable chair was placed for him close to the fire.

In those long ago times, not only were there no radios, no moving pictures, no television; there were also no story books. The greatest pleasure for everyone, old or young, was to listen to the verses which a *skald* might recite for them.

A *skald's* stories were usually filled with excitement. So well did he speak his words that he made the old Norse giants and gods and kings seem alive again. It was just like a play. Girls smiled at his tales of princesses who might even have been the daughters of gods. Boys held their breath as they listened to the daring deeds of Viking heroes who roamed those stormy north seas.

What adventures those sea-rovers met in their raids upon other lands! What battles they fought! And what rich treasures they captured! How could the Viking ships come safely through the tempests the *skald* told about?

It was in Denmark that these wandering poets most often recited this tale of the Little King on the Viking Ship. For that Little King once ruled that land. Some say he was the very first king of the Danes.

It happened in a time long before anyone can remember. Denmark had no king at all then. There was no law in the land. No one had power to punish brigands and bandits. The rich gave but little thought to the needs of the poor. And almost everyone quarreled with his neighbor next door. O, that was a very bad time for the Danes.

"If only we had a king! A wise king, a brave king, a king with a good heart! A king is what we need." The people of Denmark spoke thus to each other. But they could never agree where this king could be found.

It was fishermen on the seashore who one fine day first

spied the strange Viking ship. It was a splendid ship, painted bright red. Red, too, was the color of its square sail. A proud, golden dragon raised its head from its prow. And twenty round shining shields were hung on each of its sides.

The news of the strange red ship spread quickly along that Danish shore. Fishermen put down their nets. Women and children ran out of their houses. Viking warriors gathered. All wanted to watch that scarlet ship ride the waves up onto the sand.

From what land the red ship had come, no one could tell. What manner of men would come over its sides? There was fear in the hearts of the throng there on the beach.

But no man rose from the steering oar. No captain stood by the mast. No one at all came ashore from that scarlet vessel.

"Where are the bold Vikings who surely must have brought this ship over the sea? Why are they hiding? Do they mean to surprise us during the night?" These were the questions in everyone's mind.

Always, in those times so long ago, there was danger from enemies from over the sea. The Danes themselves often sailed forth from their own shores for such a conquest.

One day, two days, three days the people waited there on the beach for some sign of life on that Viking ship.

"Come forth, O Vikings!" the Danish men shouted. "Come forth and fight us like true warriors." Again and again they called. But there was no answer.

"Are you afraid, Strangers, now that you are so far from home?" The Danes thought jeers like this might bring forth the proud sea-rovers. Still there was no reply.

"We shall have to board the ship ourselves to solve this riddle." It was the leader of the Danes who spoke sensibly at last.

"Yes, go aboard!" the crowd shouted eagerly.

So, with their swords and their daggers and even their battle-axes in their hands, a party of warriors bravely boarded the ship. With all these weapons they must have felt a bit silly when they found no one there at all except a baby boy.

The child lay on a silken cushion, smiling in his sleep. A bundle of golden wheat was his pillow. A rich silken banner hung above his head. And about him, on all sides, was piled a cargo fit for a king.

The bottom of that scarlet ship was covered with treasures. The heaps of glittering arms made the Danes' eyes open wide. Golden swords with sharp points of gleaming ivory were there. Bronze weapons decorated with wolves' teeth and boars' teeth, with amber and agate! Daggers and spears of bronze, overlaid with gold! Axes and bows as tall as a man! Shields of all kinds were piled on the seats of the oarsmen. Never had these Danes seen such splendid coats of mail, nor helmets that shone so brightly.

"Here is the booty of a hundred victorious Viking raids," one Dane cried. "Surely this is a sign of victory for us."

"See the silken gowns! The rich mantles of fur! Look at

[178]

these flutes, these harps, and these horns!" another cried "And the new wheat under the baby's head! All these foretell riches which the child will bring us."

"This young child is sent to us by the gods to be our king," the bold leader of the boarding party cried to the crowds when he carried the baby among them.

Everyone marveled at the sleeping infant. What else but a miracle of the gods could have brought it alone over the sea? Who else but the gods could have sent such treasures as were brought out over the sides of the ship?

"Long live our baby king! May he grow to be a wise ruler!" Shouts came from all sides.

It was decided that his name should be "Skiold," which means a shield. "As a shield shall our baby king protect us from our foes!" The happy Danes cheered.

The little King from the Viking ship grew into a handsome youth. As strong and as fearless as the boldest Viking warrior was he. That could be said of him long before he was grown.

There was the time of which the *skald* sang, when Skiold fought with a bear. It was during a hunt, and the youth had strayed away from his party. Alone in the deep forest he walked, looking for game.

Suddenly, out of a thicket, a huge bear sprang upon him. With its hairy arms spread, the beast rushed at the youth.

Although he had no sword nor battle-axe to protect him, Skiold gave no cry. He did not run away. Instead he dropped his bow and grappled with the bear. Matching his strength against that of the beast, he wrestled with all his might. It must have been a fearsome sight, the young King in fierce contest with such a huge bear.

When the hunting party arrived, searching for their missing King, the bear lay on the ground, panting and weak. Skiold was holding him there with one foot on the beast's head. The spears of the hunters quickly finished him off.

This young King was but sixteen years old when he led his country's army into battle. The enemy was a strong neighbor nation, the people known as the Saxons. Who would have thought that so young a warrior could have won a glorious victory over such a strong foe.

When the two armies came together it was decided that a duel between their two leaders should settle the matter. This is the way the *skalds* sang about it:

> *"Their shields gleamed like the sun.*
> *Their swords flashed like the lightning.*
> *Where in all the wide world*
> *was there ever such daring?*
>
> *"But the Saxon Duke, Skat,*
> *Was no match for Young Skiold.*
> *He was brought to his knees*
> *And his land made a vassal.*
>
> *" 'That our peace may endure,'*
> *So spoke the young Danish hero,*
> *'I will choose for my dear bride*
> *The Saxon King's own fair daughter.' "*

Many were the other songs about the greatness of Denmark's King Skiold. All through the north countries he stood as a king among kings. Good was he, and just. He looked after the poor and he cared for the sick. No other ruler could match him in the love his people felt for him.

Well, at last there came a day when Skiold was old and fell ill. Death was near, and he called his people about him.

"Beloved subjects," he said, "I shortly must leave you. When that time comes, I would go away from you in this manner.

"My scarlet ship waits for me in a cove down on the seashore. There you will find it, the very same ship which brought me to you. Only now my ship's dragon prow is turned to face the broad sea.

"When my eyes close for the last time, lay me down on my ship's boards. Place my crown on my head and my sword by my side. Then let my ship bear me away over the sea to the Other World."

There was weeping throughout the land when the King died. But his commands were obeyed. On a silken couch near the ship's mast they laid him, dressed in his most splendid royal robes. By his side they placed his sword, which had brought such glory to their land. A bundle of yellow wheat pillowed his head. A bright silken banner was hung over his couch.

For two days and two nights his people filed past Skiold to bid him farewell. Each one brought a parting gift for his use in that Other World. Warriors laid down their swords, their daggers, their bows and arrows. Women placed on his breast their most shining jewels. Each gave of his best. And those who had nothing better to give decked his couch with sweet blossoms from their humble gardens. When it sailed away, as when it arrived, Skiold's ship held a cargo fit for a king.

Its red sail was unfurled. The shields on its sides were bright in the afternoon sun. A hundred sad warriors waded out into the water to give it a gentle push out onto the sea.

All the Danes on the sandy shore dropped to their knees. And they prayed to their gods for a fair wind to follow their King on his last voyage.

From that time on, when death came, many brave Vikings set sail into the sunset, just like King Skiold. While they were alive, their finest adventures had been on the sea. At the end of their lives, what more could they ask than just one last voyage in their beloved ship?

Beowulf Fights a Battle with the Sea

*M*ORE THAN ONE THOUSAND YEARS AGO, AN ENGLISH poet told the story of a great hero from Sweden whose name was Beowulf. People who read that story today still marvel at the courage and boldness of this splendid young man. How he sailed from his own country across the Kattegat Sea to save his neighbors, the Danes, from a man-eating giant! How with his own hands he killed that monster! And how he destroyed the giant's fierce mother who lived on the bottom of a deep lake!

A fine, handsome youth was this Beowulf. His father was King of the people called Geats, who lived in Southern Sweden. And of all the young princes in his part of the world, Beowulf was the bravest and strongest.

"His hand has the strength of thirty strong men," people there said of him. Many young warriors were glad to sail under his leadership when he set forth for Denmark.

The man-eating giant was a monster called Grendel.

Each night, for more than twelve years, he had crept into the fine banquet hall of the Danish King, Hrothgar, and killed all he found there.

Nowhere in all the world was there such a magnificent hall. Its walls were covered with gold plate and inlaid with ivory. Splendid feasts could be held there. But small use did King Hrothgar have of it except in the daytime. With the dark would come the monster, Grendel, and the guests at the feasts would have to run for their lives.

So it was a warm welcome that King Hrothgar gave the young Geat Prince, Beowulf, when he announced he had come to do battle with Grendel.

"God has sent you to aid us," the Danish King said to the young hero. "May you have success! But many others have failed. My best warriors have perished when they awaited the monster. Only their blood on the floor of my banquet hall was left to tell the story the next morning. The sharpest swords do not kill Grendel. No matter how many attack him, he is the victor."

"I have killed giants before. I have destroyed monsters of the ocean. With my own hands I will conquer this demon against whom sharp swords have no power."

Everyone in Hrothgar's court cheered Beowulf's brave words. They knew of the fame of this bold Swedish Prince. The golden banquet hall rang with his praises.

But there was one young Prince, Unferth, a favorite of the King, who had no praise for the hero.

"You speak boldly, Beowulf." He raised his voice so all

could hear. "Are you so sure of the victory over this Grendel? Are you always the victor? I should not say so.

"Think back to your battle in the sea with the brave youth called Breca. He bested you there in the ocean waves. He made his way safely to Norway's shores, while you were not to be found."

The courtiers at the banquet table were astounded to hear these unfriendly words spoken by Unferth.

"Unferth has drunk too much. He is jealous of the young hero. He does not like the idea that this Swedish Prince should succeed when he himself has not had the courage to try." These were the whispers that went round the tables.

Beowulf then answered him in a loud ringing voice.

"You do not speak fairly, friend Unferth," he cried. "Breca did not win our contest in the sea. Our goal was to determine who could brave the stormy waves longer. Which one of us two proved the stronger? Listen, O King, and judge for yourself."

It was not that Beowulf wished to boast of his strength and his victory. It was that the King should hear the truth so that he would give him permission to try his might against Grendel. He wanted to guard that fateful banquet hall without help from the king's men.

"We were boys, Breca and I," Beowulf began his tale to the banqueters. "Our friends said we were foolish to battle with the ocean. But we wanted to match our strength, one against the other. And where better should we do this than in the wild waves of the sea?

"We would swim side by side out into the ocean. We would wear our golden corselets to protect our bodies from the teeth of sea monsters. And in one hand, each of us would carry a sharp, shining sword.

"It was I who swam faster. But it was our bargain that we should stay close together. And I did not leave Breca behind.

"For five days and five nights we fought against the great ocean. Storms tossed us about like small bits of wood.

"Sea monsters attacked us, and it was my sword which killed no less than nine. How many did Breca kill?" Beowulf asked the question of Unferth, who, ashamed now, turned his eyes away.

"Breca killed none. When the sun shone after the storm, all the nine monsters whose dead bodies floated in to the shore, had been killed by my sword.

"One of those sea giants almost destroyed me." The banquet guests forgot to eat, so spellbound were they.

"The great monster seized my legs in his great jaws," Beowulf continued. He pulled me down, down, and down to the very sea bottom. He would have devoured me had my sword not found his heart.

"It was in the midst of a tempest that Breca and I were at last driven apart. I saw no more of him. But I heard he found his way safely that day to the Norway coast nearby.

"My strength was greater. It carried me on and on through the sea to far away Lapland.

"Doubt my courage and skill if you will, Unferth." Beowulf was ending his brave speech at the banquet table. "But one who has killed nine sea monsters should have no trouble with even such a one as Grendel. I shall face him without fear, if the King gives me permission."

Shouts then filled the great room. And Hrothgar gave the order that the young hero from Sweden should keep guard there that night and try his might against the monster, Grendel.

Morning proved that this Beowulf had not been just boasting. He had spoken what was true. For the man-eating monster lay dead there in the King's banquet hall. With his bare hands the young man from over the sea had slain the beast. By himself, Beowulf had freed Hrothgar and his people from Grendel's twelve-year-old curse.

There was still another battle, however, for Beowulf to win. This was with the monster's mother who came to avenge her son. She was as bloodthirsty as Grendel had been. And before he had killed her, the young hero had followed her to her palace on the floor of a deep lake.

Here, a second underwater battle took place. Clad in his golden coat of mail, and with a shining helmet to cover his head, Beowulf fought. There on the lake bottom, with his magic sword he cut off the creature's ugly head. And her blood stained the waters of that lake a deep red.

Songs were sung of the bravery of the young Geat Prince. Rich treasures were loaded upon his ship when he was ready to set sail for his homeland. Jewels and rings there were. Horses and armor, and plates of beaten gold! All these Beowulf took back to his father, the King of the Geats.

Many were the other victories of which the English poet tells in his story of Beowulf. But none was more magnificent than his victory over Grendel, nor indeed—for it happened when he was only a boy—than his victory over his friend, Breca, in their battle with the sea.

The Cowskin Boat

THE LONG-AGO TIMES WERE TIMES OF MAGIC AND mystery, so our grandmothers say. Young men were brave. And young girls were fair.

You had to be careful then, just the same. The bravest young man might turn out to be a wizard. The fairest young girl might be a witch.

Animals talked, then, in the words of men. And fairies, both bad and good, were found in the most unlikely places.

Now, who would have thought that a cow could work magic? Who ever would have believed that a cow's skin could uncover a mystery?

Surely Pedro, the Chilean boy, never did. Nor did his father, Juan, nor his mother, Rosa, nor his little sister, Marita.

The rancho by the sea on which Pedro and his family lived was small. Only three cows ate the green grass of its meadow. Only seven sheep were there to give wool for weaving the ponchos to keep them warm in the cold weather.

Still, there was usually enough to eat in the low rancho house. Every one in that family was happy and gay until the fair young girl came to live on the rancho next door.

After she arrived, strange things began to happen. Animals disappeared and never were found.

"Surely she is a witch, for all she is so fair," the neighbors said. "Surely she has the Devil himself for a friend." For they had heard the sounds of strange merrymaking in the dark of the moon on the rancho where she lived.

Well, witch or no witch, it was after she came that Pedro's father, Juan, began to take his sheep and cows to the market.

First the white cow went away. And what Juan did with the money he got for her, nobody knew.

Then the black cow went to market. Where Juan put her price his wife, Rosa, could not find out.

The next week the brown cow was led down the road.

"What will our children do?" Rosa said sadly. "At least bring back a nanny goat, Juan. Pedro and Marita must have milk of some kind to drink." Tears stood in her eyes while she watched the man and the cow walk out of her sight.

Tears rolled down her cheeks that evening, tears and more tears. For neither the brown cow nor her master came back to the rancho. The sun set. The stars shone. Yet Juan did not return.

All the night, Rosa watched. Then, with the dawn, the brown cow came home, all by herself.

"Here is something strange!" Rosa cried out to her neighbors. "Our brown cow has come home. The rope still hangs round her horns. But her sides drip with salt water as if she had been in the sea. And my good Juan is not with her."

The neighbors shook their heads. No one could understand what had happened until there came, riding by, a man who lived on the seashore.

"I saw your husband last evening, as the sun set," he said to Rosa. "He was riding on a black horse and he was leading the brown cow. The witch girl sat behind him on the black horse's back. They rode that black horse right into the sea, but the brown cow broke loose."

Then did the tears stream down poor Rosa's face. Then was she sure a witch's spell was on her dear husband. She went about her rancho with a heavy heart.

Pedro helped his mother as much as he could. He took the brown cow to their meadow down by the sea. And he cared for his little sister, Marita, at the same time.

One day Pedro's mother went in to the town to sell her butter and cream. She left the boy and the little girl playing safely on the seashore. The brown cow was safe, too, eating green grass in their meadow nearby. It was midsummer and the weather was hot.

"Let's go wading, Marita," said Pedro. "The sea water will cool our feet."

The little girl beamed. It was fun to splash in the gentle waves that rolled up on the sand. Marita laughed when she tried to catch up some of the white foam in her small hands.

Then, all at once, there came a giant wave. It knocked the two children down. It rolled them over and over, over and over.

Like a ball, Pedro was thrown about in the rough water. Then somehow he got up again on his feet. At once he looked for Marita. But Marita was not there.

"Marita! Marita!" Pedro ran into the waves, which now were just as calm as before. He swam out from the shore, and he dived under the water. But he could not find his small sister.

Panting, he threw himself down on the sand. And he wept as if his heart would break.

Then a soft, low voice spoke into his ear.

"Do not cry, Ninyo!* You may yet find Marita."

The boy looked about him. No one was there. No one but the brown cow which had come home alone from the seashore the day his father disappeared.

"Dry your tears, Ninyo!" It was indeed the brown cow that was speaking to him. "Dry your tears and listen! The witch girl took your father away. The witch girl took your sister. Your turn will come next unless you do just what I say."

*Little One

[196]

"What must I do, Cow?" The boy did not know what to think of a cow that could talk.

"You must take off my skin. Throw it down on the water! Then climb onto it as if it were a wooden raft. Cling fast to my tail! Whenever you are in danger, pull out one of the hairs. And help will come."

"Above all, my Pedro," the brown cow went on talking, "take care to put my two eyes into your pocket. With them you will be able to look far across the broad ocean. You can see the tops of high mountains. You can see through thick stone walls."

Somehow or other Pedro got the cow's skin off. He did not forget to put her eyes in his pocket.

Then he threw the cow's skin down on the waves, and he jumped upon it. Holding tight to the tail, the boy floated away in his cowskin boat far, far from the shore.

That was a strange journey. Once a hundred big, ugly fish swam in a ring around his cowskin boat. They came closer and closer. They tried to pull the cowskin boat down under the waves.

"Surely I am in danger now," Pedro thought. "I must pull a hair out of the cow's tail."

At once that hair turned into a long wooden oar. With it, Pedro could beat upon the heads of the ugly fish. One by one, he killed them all. Then his cowskin boat could float on.

Another time there flew down from the sky a flock of huge birds. Great black birds they were, with cruel sharp beaks. And one after another they lit on the edge of the cow's skin. They were so heavy that Pedro's small boat began to sink into the water.

"Danger is here again," the boy cried aloud. He pulled a second hair from the cow's tail. And in his hands he found he was holding a gun, ready to shoot.

With this gun, the boy easily killed the giant black birds. His cowskin boat floated away, once more, in peace.

Pedro had come far, when thick blocks of ice formed in the water all round his boat. They were packed so tight together that it could not move.

This time the boy was so frightened that he pulled a whole tuft of magic hairs from the cow's tail. Some of the hairs fell on the ice cakes, and at once they became blazing bonfires. They melted the ice cakes, and then the sea was clear.

Now and then Pedro took the cow's eyes out of his pocket. With them to look through, he could watch birds fly as high as the sun. He could see fish swim on the sea bottom. He could look far, O, very far across the blue waves.

"Ai, there is an island! And there is a castle upon it!" Pedro cried out to himself. "It is a tall castle with thick walls of stone. And what is that I see inside those stone walls?"

You have guessed, I am sure, that Pedro saw in that castle his beloved sister and his lost father. But have you guessed, too, that he saw the witch girl?

His father, Juan, was in chains. He was made fast to a tall black stone in the very center of the castle hall. His face was turned aside. He would not look at the knife in the hands of the wicked witch girl. For she was holding it close to the heart of his daughter, Marita.

"Now, indeed, it is the time to use hairs from my cow's tail." Pedro did not wait. He laid one of the magic hairs against the high castle wall. Straightway it turned into a ladder, which led him to a window that was wide open.

In the wink of an eye, Pedro jumped in through the window in the castle wall. He landed neatly upon the witch girl. The knife fell from her hand when she dropped to the floor.

It was easy for Pedro to tie the hands and feet of the stunned witch. It was a strong rope which the magic hairs made for him, and she could not break loose.

It was easy, too, for the boy to unfasten the chains that held his father fast. The man wept for joy when he threw his arms about his dear son and his little daughter.

As Pedro could see with the cow's magic eyes, there was a hidden door and a staircase that led down from beside the black rock in the center of the castle hall. The steps curved about, going on and on far down under the earth.

Together, the man and the boy rolled the wicked witch to the top of these steps. There they gave her a push. They heard her shrill cries. Then all was still and they knew she could never harm them again.

Pedro and his father, with Marita safe in his arms, made their way down those steps. Halfway to the bottom, they came to the open door of the witch's treasure room.

It would not be a proper tale at all if they had not found in it gold coins and diamonds, silver pieces and emeralds and other fine jewels. All were there for them to gather up and take away.

They heaped the cowskin boat with these treasures. The more they piled on, the bigger the boat seemed to become. Then they climbed aboard, all three, and set forth for home.

There, on the seashore, they found poor Rosa. Her eyes were red from weeping, and from looking and looking for her husband and her children. What joy there was in her face when the lost ones told their tale! And how everyone cried out at the dangers Pedro had faced!

"It was our good brown cow." Pedro had tears in his eyes when he spoke of her. "It was her magic that saved us. Alas, she is gone! But we can at least bury her bones."

The boy spread out the cow's skin. His father helped him to place on it the body of the brown cow, which still lay on the sand. Pedro did not forget to put in the cow's eyes. He even remembered the magic hairs from her tail, which were still in his pocket.

Wonder of wonders! No sooner had the magic hairs touched the cow's body than she rose from the ground, in her own skin, as well and fat as before.

Do you believe this tale? I'm not sure that I do. But I

like the idea of the witch girl being punished and the brown
cow coming to life again.

We must not forget about the gold and the silver and
the witch's jewels. With such riches Juan could have many
meadows. He could buy more sheep and more cows. But
I'm sure the brown cow was put into the best of the meadows
to graze.

Each year when the neighbors came to help get the cows
ready for the market, Pedro hung a wreath of bright flowers
over her horns. There was no danger then that someone
might drive his dear brown cow away from the rancho with
the other beasts.

The Eight Perfect Ones
on the Ocean

*I*N MOST HOMES IN ANCIENT CHINA ONE COULD FIND THE "Eight Who Live Forever," sometimes called also "The Eight Perfect Ones."

They might be painted on teapots or fans, on wooden chests or paper scrolls. They might be embroidered on silk coats, or wall hangings, or covers for beds. Or their likenesses might be figures of ivory, or bronze, or of smooth shining wood.

In those days every Chinese boy and girl knew the story of "The Eight Who Live Forever." It was an exciting tale. The Eight could fly through the air on the clouds, or walk on the sea. Together these seven men and one maiden traveled far over the earth, up into the air, even down under the waves. The Eight Perfect Ones and their magic would surely bring a house good luck.

What a strange company they were!

A doctor with an iron crutch who carried a gourd filled with magic medicine.

A hermit whose feather fan was a reminder that a stork had once taken him to the Heavenly Kingdom of the Gods.

A singer with a sweet flute and a pair of shining cymbals.

A magician who rode on a mule made out of paper which he could fold up and put away in his pocket.

A beautiful maiden whose homes were on the highest mountain peaks, and whose flower was the lotus.

A dragon-killer with his magic sword, and his fly brush for sweeping the clouds from the sky.

A poet who wrote verses on the petals of flowers.

A prince who carried with him a tablet from the Emperor, the Son of Heaven, himself.

These were the Eight Perfect Ones in the old legend which was told so often in Old China. There is a story about each one which tells how the Gods made him perfect and gave him the magic gift of living forever. But the story I have for you here is about all the Eight, and how they once fought a battle with the Dragon King of the Eastern Sea.

"Let us explore the realms of the sea dragons," one of the Eight suggested on a fine summer morning. "We have gone far over the earth. We have ridden across the sky. Now let us see the wonders that lie under the waves."

"We could travel above the ocean upon a low cloud and look down through the water to the sea bottom." This was proposed by another one of the group.

"No," said a third, "let us keep close to the ocean. Let each one throw down the treasure he carries with him upon the water and let him ride upon it."

This was a better idea, they agreed. The doctor stood on his iron crutch as if it were a surfboard. The hermit rode on his feather fan as safely as he had flown up to heaven on the back of his stork. The paper mule was unfolded and rode upon the water as sure as a raft.

And so it was also with the flower basket of the poet, the flute of the singer, the magic sword, the lotus flower, and the Emperor's tablet.

Some pictures of these Eight Perfect Ones show seven sitting close together in a small boat. The magician on his paper mule is riding behind over the waves. But even in such pictures each of the Eight has his special treasure with him.

What wonders the Eight saw when they gazed down at the sea bottom! By their magic they could look into the very palaces of the Dragon Kings of the Sea. Five of these shining palaces there were. One stood on the very center of the ocean floor. It was the palace of the Supreme Water Dragon. The other four were in the east, the west, the north, and the south.

All five were magnificent. Like rainbows were the colored stones in their walls. Crystal-clear were the doors which led into the courts of the Dragon Kings. Opals and pearls and other fine gems were everywhere.

One sea journey which the Eight planned was a visit to the God of Long Life. His home was far, far away across the Eastern Sea.

It was to this God that the Eight owed their magic gift of living forever. So it was fitting that they should take with them fine presents to celebrate the day of his birth.

"We must have a servant to carry our birthday gifts to the God of Long Life," said one of the Eight. In the China of long ago, important people always had servants to prepare their way and to bear their burdens.

"But," another objected, "how shall a servant, without our magic power, walk on the ocean?" This indeed was a problem.

The Eight solved it by making a small raft of cypress wood. They built it just big enough to carry the servant and the treasures for the God of Long Life. And they tied it behind their own magic boat.

Gaily they set forth to cross the wide Eastern Sea. They could pass the time looking down at the wonders of the underwave world. And the Sea Dragons, for their part, could look up through the clear water and watch the strange travelers. They could see all the rich gifts that were piled on their raft.

No doubt some of the dragons of the sea would have

liked for themselves the ripe, juicy peaches-of-long-life upon it. Perhaps they wanted, too, the flute and the cymbals, and the sword which they saw in the boat with the Eight. At least that is what the Perfect Ones said when the storm came.

"Surely it is the Sea Dragon King who sends this storm upon us," they decided, as they watched the waves rise. "Only powerful sea spirits could throw water so high into the air. Only they could blow winds strong enough to overturn our raft." With dismay, the Eight watched their servant and their gifts for the God of Long Life spilled into the ocean.

"We shall complain of this to the Dragon King of this Eastern Sea," cried the doctor with the iron crutch. He pointed the open neck of his medicine gourd down at the water. And a light brighter than the sun was sent by its magic along the sea bottom. Like a searchlight, it traveled until it shone into the palace of the Dragon King.

The King of the Eastern Sea was alarmed by the strange fiery light, and he sent one of his courtiers to the surface of the water to find out what it meant.

"Your master, the Dragon King, has blown a hurricane upon our boat. He has turned over our raft, and spilled our servant and our treasures into the ocean. We are angry, indeed." So the Eight made their complaint. And they also made their demand for fair treatment.

"The Dragon King must return to us alive our servant who now is a prisoner inside his palace. He must set our raft straight and put back upon it our birthday gifts for the God of Long Life."

The Eight Perfect Ones had faith in the power of their own magic. They dared to speak firmly to the Sea King's messenger. And their words were repeated to the ruler of the ocean in his underwave home.

"It was not I who sent the hurricane upon these good travelers. Who did this evil thing?" The Dragon King questioned each one in his court. And it was discovered that the storm-raiser had indeed been his own son. The greedy Dragon Prince had wanted the treasures on the cypress-wood raft for himself.

His father's anger did not make the Prince send back the servant and the gifts for the raft. He only gathered together some other young dragons and set forth to do battle with the Eight Perfect Ones.

Now the magic of those undersea dragons was great. But the magic of the Eight Favorites of the Gods was even greater. The Prince's great teeth and his sharp sword had not enough power to harm them.

The Singer at once changed his magic flute into a giant fishing rod. And when the Dragon Prince swam near, he was neatly caught on its hook and made a prisoner.

"Go back to the Dragon King," the Perfect Ones told the other young dragons. "Tell him we shall hold his son until our servant comes back to us alive, and our treasures are put safely again on our raft."

"My son is in the wrong," the Sea Dragon King said. "Let the servant be restored! Let the gifts be returned!"

But in the underwave kingdom, there were officials who did not agree with the King. They dared to object.

"The Eight are too bold," they cried. "They dare hold our royal Prince as a common prisoner. And all because of a lowly servant and a few trinkets. They have insulted Your Majesty. They must feel the power of the Great King of the Eastern Sea or he will 'lose face.'"

Now, in old China, to lose face was to lower oneself in the eyes of the world. And no ruler wanted that. So the Dragon King was persuaded. He called up his army and prepared for the battle.

By means of the doctor's magic gourd and its searchlight, the Eight saw what was happening on the sea bottom. They called on their Gods. And they summoned all the other Perfect Ones, who, like themselves, had received the gift of strong magic.

It was a strange battle. A ball of fire was hurled by one of the Heavenly Gods upon the head of the Dragon King himself. Magic rain fell from Heaven into the sea. Its power was so strong that the warriors of the Dragon King became as weak as the small fishes that swam harmlessly all around the boat of the Eight.

The noise of the battle, however, came to the ears of the Supreme Water Dragon. That one ruled the ocean, the lakes, the ponds, and all the waters in the world. The Sea

Dragons obeyed him, and now he summoned to his palace the guilty King of the Eastern Sea. There was anger in his voice as he reproved him.

"You were wicked to make war upon the Eight Perfect Ones who are beloved by the Gods. Give back their treasures at once. Restore life to their servant. If I should report you to the Great One who rules the Universe, surely he would remove you from your Eastern Sea throne. Surely he would have for you a punishment to remember."

So the servant came up alive from under the waves. The raft was put right side up again in the water. And the birthday gifts were once more piled safely upon it. Gaily, again, the Eight went along on their journey to greet the God of Long Life.

In the fairy tales of some lands, there is magic in the number three. In those of other lands it may be seven. But in the China of the old fairy tales, it is the number eight.

Always, the stories of the Eight Perfect Ones ended happily, for them at least. Perhaps that is why in China this number has stood for good luck. Perhaps that is why, also, artists and sculptors and those who embroidered on silk liked to put the Eight Who Live Forever into their designs.

The Monkey Bridge

*I*N A BENARES GARDEN, ONE DAY LONG AGO, A BROWN-skinned Indian boy squatted down on the terrace to feed a small monkey.

"Hanuman has come to visit me again, Amrita," he said to his sister, who stood watching him.

Of all the monkeys that lived in the courts of the Hindu temple nearby, Ramu liked this one the best. These yellow beasts, with their funny black faces and black feet, ran freely over the housetops and garden walls of this holy Hindu city of Benares.

Most of the monkeys were gentle and tame. They seemed sure that people were friendly. But the bright-eyed creature which Ramu was feeding that day was the tamest, the gentlest one of them all. It would eat from the boy's hand. It liked to sit on his shoulder and curl his tail round

Ramu's neck. It even allowed a blue glass ring from the Benares bazaar to be put on its furry arm.

"I call this one Hanuman because he is my friend, just as the real Hanuman, the Monkey King, was the friend of Rama for who I am named," Ramu told his sister.

In India, then, many boys were given the name of this god-prince, whose story has been told there for hundreds of years. Their mothers hoped, no doubt, that the name Rama might bring to their sons some of that ancient hero's courage and goodness.

No prince among the Hindu gods of earliest times was more handsome than Rama. Some said he had the face and the body of the Great God, Vishnu, himself. No young man was stronger. None was more skillful in handling the royal elephants.

Just as Rama had the form of Vishnu, greatest of all Gods, so a certain princess named Sita was said to have the face and form of Vishnu's fair wife. Her beauty was so great that many young princes and gods wanted her for their wife.

The test for Sita's bridegroom was that he should be strong enough to bend the giant bow of the four-faced shining God, Brahma. It took five thousand men to draw the cart upon which Brahma's bow was brought forth for the trials. One prince, then another, tried to lift it out of its case. But each one failed.

It was only when Rama laid his hands upon it that the

bow could be lifted. Rama drew back its bowstring. He sent its great arrow to the ends of the earth. With a sound like the thunder, the bow was snapped like a twig by Rama's great strength.

So Sita became the bride of the god-prince, Rama. And a perfect wife she was. At many a wedding in India today, her name is still spoken. Her song is sung, and all recall the words she spoke when her young husband was wrongfully sent into exile in the deep forest.

Rama begged Sita to wait for him until his exile was over. He did not want her to suffer the hardships he would have to bear wandering through the wilderness and sleeping on the ground.

"Stay here in comfort in my father's palace, dear Sita," he pleaded. But she would not.

"*A loyal wife,*" she softly cried,
"*Will never leave her husband's side.*"

This was the theme of Sita's song, which still is heard in India today.

So Sita went with Rama into the deep forest. Happily she feasted with him upon roots and wild fruits. Together they slept under the trees and bathed in the brooks. And they were as content to be there with each other, as they had been when he was still a prince in a palace.

"My only fear is that the Demon, Ravana, will take you away from me," Rama said to his dear bride. "Ravana's great joy is to torment men like me. He is a wife-stealer, and he has carried away the bride of many a prince. Always, always, my dear one, beware of the Demon, Ravana."

This Ravana was so strong that it took twenty arms to hold his great muscles. He was so clever that he had ten different heads. The Gods themselves could not kill him. Thunderbolts had been hurled at him. Heavenly birds and magic serpents had been sent to wound him.

His battles with the Gods had left ugly scars on his ten faces. But he had not been destroyed.

It was by a trick that Ravana at last succeeded in carrying off the beautiful Sita. One day a golden deer appeared to her in the forest. Its horns were bright as jewels. Its ears were as delicate as sea shells. And its coat was soft and smooth like a lotus petal. How could such a lovely creature do any one harm?

But Rama knew better.

"Do not pet that deer, Beloved," the Prince warned his bride. "It may be one of Ravana's demons in a deer's form."

Rama ran to get his bow and his arrows. And he chased the golden deer far, far into the deep woods.

It was while he was gone that the Demon, Ravana, came to Sita. At first he appeared in the form of a Holy Man. And he offered the young wife of Rama a rich house and a sweet-scented garden if she would go with him.

When she would not, the Holy Man was changed before her eyes into the dread Demon with his ten heads and

[218]

twenty arms. In a breath, he had seized her and had thrown her into his flying chariot. And they were gone from that forest.

Rama's cries rang through the trees, when he found his bride gone. The animals grieved with him. Jackals howled. Hyenas screamed. Birds sang mournful songs.

The young hero asked every living creature he came upon for news of his wife. Animals then were as clever as men. They often came to the aid of their two-legged brothers.

It was old Jatayu, the vulture, who finally told Rama where Sita had gone.

"I flew to aid her, but Ravana was too strong for me," the ancient bird said. "He knocked me from the side of his flying chariot. I followed as fast as I could and I saw the jewels and veils which Sita threw out so that you might trace her. They lead over the ocean to Ravana's Island of Lanka." Lanka was the name then of Ceylon, which lies across the wide waters of the Indian Ocean.

The news was bad for Prince Rama. How should he cross the miles of ocean water which lay between him and his dear wife? How should he alone fight Ravana and his army of demons?

"I shall seek help from my brothers, the Monkey Kings," he decided at last. "Sugriva, King of all the Monkey Tribes, is my good friend. Sugriva is wise. He knows the ways of the demons. And his magic is strong. With help from the Monkey Kings, I shall rescue my wife."

Now it was indeed Sugriva who called forth the vast

monkey army to fight at the side of this noble Prince. From east, west, north, and south the beasts came, leaping by the thousands, even by the millions.

But it was a lesser Monkey King, Hanuman, who helped Rama the most, as you shall see.

The monkey scouts had searched for a way to reach Lanka to the east, to the west, and to the north. But they had found none. In the south, too, which was the nearest, they were stopped by the wide ocean.

"How shall we ever cross the broad waters of this sea?" The monkeys were awed by the vastness of the Indian Ocean.

"I will leap across the wide water," Hanuman cried boldly. He took his stand on the top of a high, high mountain peak. There he prayed to the Sun and to his father, the Wind God. Before the eyes of the watchers, he began to grow larger. Larger and larger he grew, until he was as big as a giant.

Hanuman's eyes flashed like the lightning. He roared like the thunder. His great tail waved like a battle flag as he jumped into the air. With one mighty bound he reached the shores of the Island of Lanka. And there he took on again his own size and form.

When he came to the gate of the great city where Ravana's palace was, Hanuman made himself smaller, as small as a cat. No one noticed him as he searched the Demon's palace for the fair Sita.

Under an asoka tree in the walled garden, she sat under

the watchful eyes of her demon guards. She seemed thin and sad, but she had not been badly treated.

"I come from Ramu," the Monkey said, joining his paws and bowing before her in a proper Indian salute. "I am here to take you back over the water."

Sita would not believe this until he showed her a ring which she knew to be Rama's. But even then she was afraid to ride on his back across the deep water. "Rama will have to come for me himself," she declared.

The demon guards gave the alarm when they discovered Hanuman talking with the Princess Sita.

"We cannot kill this Monkey, because he comes to us from another king." Ravana knew how it should be between one king and another. "But we can set fire to his tail and let him burn to death."

The wicked demons bound up the Monkey's tail in dry cotton. Then they soaked it in oil and set it on fire.

"Help Hanuman, Fire God!" Sita prayed aloud. "Blaze, but do not burn Rama's friend, Hanuman!"

Her prayer was answered. Only the hair on that monkey's tail burned. But it made a fine blaze, and as he ran through the streets of the city, house after house was set on fire.

On the seashore, the Monkey King dipped his burning tail into the water and the fire was put out. Then he jumped back over the Indian Ocean to tell Rama the good news that Sita was alive and well.

At the head of his monkey army, Rama marched to the shore of the southernmost tip of India.

"Now I will pray the God of the Ocean to part the waters so that we may march safely to the Island of Lanka," the good Prince told his generals. He lay himself down upon a grass prayer mat, and for three days he prayed. But the Ocean God gave no sign that he had heard.

Then Rama grew angry. He shot deadly arrows into the water. These brought hurricane winds. But the Ocean God did not show himself until Rama bent the bow of the Great Brahma. Its magic arrow shook the mountains under the sea. It stirred the ocean waters into one giant whirlpool, and the sea creatures begged for mercy.

In a bright flash of lightning the Ocean God came up from his undersea kingdom.

"Noble Prince, be not angry," he cried. "It is not in my power to part the waves for you. Only a bridge can take your army to the Island of Lanka.

"But do not despair! You shall have such a bridge, and your monkey friends shall build it. While they work, I will calm my waves so that their bridge may stand firm."

And it was the monkey army which built the bridge. Some brought stones and trees to the seashore. Others set the stones firmly upon the sea bottom. Still others laid the tree trunks upon the stone base to make a floor for the bridge.

In five days, the splendid stone bridge ran in a straight line from the Indian mainland to the shores of Ceylon, or Lanka. Over many miles of water it reached. And as he had promised, the Ocean God held his waves still. The bridge did not even shake when the monkey army rushed across.

What battles were fought between the monkeys and the demons in Ravana's army! How the earth trembled! Fire circled the sun. And a rain of red blood fell out of the sky.

Demons and monkeys! And the magic of the demons was no match for the fury of Rama's four-footed friends. They bit and they scratched. They hurled stones through the air, and they felled the demons with tree trunks.

Both Rama and Hanuman once were sadly wounded. But the Monkey King managed to leap to the top of a high mountain and bring back life-giving herbs. So great was the magic of these plants that they healed not only the wounds of the Prince and himself but of all that monkey army.

The fiercest of the battles of that day took place when the God-Prince, Rama, and the Demon, Ravana, met face to face. Their bows were so huge that they touched the sky. Their arrows were sharper than the tooth of a serpent. Like tigers they fought. And the Gods looking down from their Heaven cheered while they watched Rama defeat the great Demon whom none of them could destroy.

Joyously, Rama and Sita led the monkey army back across the ocean bridge to their own land. In good time, that noble Prince's exile was ended, and he sat on his rightful throne with the fair Sita beside him.

Hanuman and his monkey army were well rewarded for

their help. For the monkey soldiers there was all the honey and fruit they could eat. And Rama commanded: "Always shall these monkey friends be welcome in the houses of men." This, so the story goes, is how it happens that monkeys have such a special place in the hearts of Hindus.

"For you, my good Hanuman, what shall be your reward?" Rama asked as he hung a chain of priceless rubies around the neck of the Monkey King.

"I beg the right to live for so long as the splendid story of Rama is told in this world." So Hanuman spoke, and so Rama ordered it.

No doubt that Monkey King is still living on some high Indian mountain peak, for, as you can see by these pages, Rama's story still is being told.

We can be sure he is not entirely forgotten in India, even in these times of fewer heroes and gods. In many far corners of that land there are temples in which there are statues of this good Monkey God. People come to them still to pay tribute to Hanuman's loyal friendship and unselfish service to his Prince.

What became of the bridge which the monkeys built? No one seems to know. Perhaps the waves of the Ocean God washed it away when Rama's army had no more need for it. There is today a line of rocks and reefs, however, in the Indian Ocean. It runs all the way from the tip of the Indian mainland to the Island of Ceylon.

Some call these rocks "Adam's Bridge." But others say they mark the line where, in those ancient times, Rama's bridge was built by the monkeys.

The Boat That
Would Not Move

*E*VERYONE ENJOYS A STORY ABOUT PEOPLE WHO ARE SO stupid that we have to laugh when we hear of their foolish doings. The tale makes us who read it feel wise and clever. We know that we would never be so silly ourselves, and that is a good feeling.

This is such a story. It comes from the Island of Celebes in the vast group of islands known as Indonesia.

The simple, brown-skinned people in this tale lived long ago on a faraway part of the Celebes seacoast. Their village of thatched huts was far from cities or towns. And they never left it except to paddle their dugout canoes up the river to hunt in the deep jungle.

These villagers did not need to be clever. In their warm part of the world, on the Equator itself, they had no use for clothes. A simple wrapping of cloth, made of pounded bark, covered their middles. And that was all they wore on their brown bodies.

Food was easy to find. There were coconuts and bread-fruit on nearby trees. Hunters brought home meat from the jungles. Fish swam in the sea. What need was there for much thinking?

One thing these people had to have was boats. But since they never traveled far, these did not have to be large.

They had learned from their fathers to shape the trunk of a coconut-palm tree into a canoe which they called a "prahu." A prahu such as they made was not a big boat, but there was room for more than one man to sit inside it and paddle along the river. If the sea was calm, a fisherman could take his prahu out on the ocean. He was safe so long as he stayed close to the shore.

Sometimes a trading canoe from one of the large Celebes towns stopped at the landing beach of this village. What a wonderful boat was this enormous prahu? It might have room for as many as twenty different paddlers.

And there was a framework of wooden poles on each side of it. The poles lay on the water like those of the boats that today are called outrigger canoes. These poles steadied the boat. They kept it from turning upside down so easily in the rough ocean waves.

"If only we had a prahu with an outrigger!" Bahu, the headman of the village always sighed when a trading prahu was pulled up on his beach. "We could load it with our coconuts. We could take them to the towns and trade them for treasures like those the giant prahus bring to us."

But no one in that small village knew how to put poles together into such an outrigger. Truly, the people there were not very clever, or they would have learned how. Other islanders did. It was said that the harbor at Makassar, the capital city of Celebes, was filled with such big outrigger canoes.

Well, one day a fearful storm roared over the sea near the Celebes village. The waves that rolled in were as high as a coconut palm. The winds blew the thatch roofs off the small houses. They bent the breadfruit trees over until they seemed to be kneeling. It was as if the trees were praying the sea demons to go away, far away. It was truly a storm to remember.

The simple village people had another reason, too, to remember that storm. For the rolling waves washed up onto their beach a fine empty prahu. No doubt in the storm its owner and his crew had been spilled out into the sea, in spite of its outrigging.

"This prahu is a gift to us from the King of the Sea." So Bahu, the headman, made it seem right that they should keep the boat.

The men of the village, and the women too, crowded around the prahu. They looked it all over. But not one crack did they see. Not one part of the outrigging had been broken. So they made a feast for the Sea God and took it for their own.

"Now we can take our coconuts to trade in the towns."
Bahu's dream was coming true.

For many days the village folk gathered up the ripe
coconuts for their journey. They made quite a pile on the
landing beach.

"Those who have the best paddles shall be the first to
go out in our big prahu," said Bahu, the headman. For, of
course, the paddles of the crew of the prahu had also been
spilled into the sea in the great storm.

Some of the lazier villagers had no proper paddles. They
used only broad squares of bark, thrust into a split pole.
But a few had good paddles, carved out of solid wood.
They were the ones chosen to take the prahu on its first
voyage.

There was excitement in that faraway village when the
time came to set forth. Men ran into each other in their
haste to pile the coconuts into the boat. Bahu, the headman, gave so many orders that no one could understand
just what he wanted.

"Come here! Go there!" Truly, Bahu was no wiser about
launching the big boat than anyone else. Though of course
he pretended he knew all about it.

"Hela! Hela! Take your places. Hold your paddles
ready," he called from his place of importance in the bow
of the prahu.

The villagers had planned to give the boat a fine launching. They beat on their skin drums. And they banged on the

[232]

gongs which they had got from the last trading prahu. The great noise they made would surely drive the sea demons away to their homes on the sea bottom.

"Hela! Hela! Paddle, now, paddle!" Bahu's voice was loud and clear.

The gongs sang and the drums were beaten. But the boat did not move. The paddles only threw into the air clouds of white sand. For the excited headman had forgotten to tell the boatmen to push their outrigger off the beach into the water.

"Anyone can make a mistake now and then," Bahu excused his silliness.

"I-a-le le-le-le! I-a-le le-le-le!" the boatmen sang together as they gave the big prahu a push that slid it down into the low water. Then they leapt aboard into their places and put their paddles to work.

But they were excited. And, indeed, they were not clever at all. For ten of them sat facing one way, while ten faced the other way. When Bahu, the headman, gave the order to "Paddle!" ten paddles pulled the boat forward, and ten pulled it backward. So of course the boat stayed in the same place.

Now what could the matter be? The men looked at their paddles. Then they looked at each other.

"This boat is bewitched," they cried to Bahu, the headman, who was as puzzled as they.

Then Bahu's eyes fell on the piles of coconuts.

"That's it," he cried gleefully. "The coconuts are too heavy there on the bottom of the prahu. We have put too many down on its boards. Let the ten in the stern lay their paddles down and lift the coconuts high off the boat's bottom." And he waved his hand in command to the ten men who had their backs to the rear of the prahu.

It was done. Ten men stood up, with coconuts in their arms.

Now again came the order from Bahu, the headman. "Hela! Hela! Paddle, now, paddle!"

The ten men who held their paddles in their hands were now all facing one way. So their paddles moved together as one. And the boat, at long last, began to move. The drums were beaten so loud that they sounded like thunder. The gongs filled the air with their singing. And the villagers cheered.

Bahu, the headman, was smiling so broadly that every tooth in his mouth showed.

"I knew at once what was wrong. Who says that the headman of this village is not wise and clever? It was the weight of the coconuts all the time that kept our prahu from moving."

Boys and girls of the Island of Celebes always laughed at this point in the story. They were much wiser than Bahu. They knew, of course, that whether the coconuts were in a pile, or held high in the arms of the boatmen, their weight was still in the prahu.

[234]

The Boat That Would Not Move

Celebes children had ridden out on the sea ever since they were small. They knew it was the paddles all going the same way that made that boat move at last.

The Miracle on
the Jaffa Sea

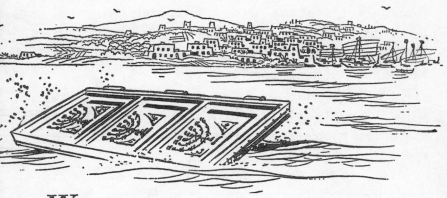

W AS IT A MIRACLE?

Or was it a sea serpent?

One or the other of these was the way people explained a strange happening on the Mediterranean Sea not many years before Christ was born.

In our times, ships made of metal travel easily over the ocean. But in ancient Bible times, no shipbuilder dreamed that a seagoing vessel could be made of heavier material than wood. That is why a huge door made of copper, silver, and gold, floating on water seemed so amazing.

A king of ancient Judea and his temple in Jerusalem! A rich merchant across the Mediterranean Sea! And a pair of copper doors on a ship in the midst of a storm! These were the three important things in this old tale. Perhaps there was a giant sea serpent also. But of that one cannot be sure. Nobody saw it.

The King was Herod, the Great. He ruled over the part of ancient Palestine known as Judea. Herod, the Maker of Beautiful Cities, he was called. And his name was praised in all the lands around the Mediterranean Sea. It was another Herod, one of this Great Herod's sons, who was King when Christ was born.

Far and wide, in those times, men talked of Herod's cities. But most of all they marveled at Jerusalem, and its magnificent temple on the high hill called the "Mountain of God."

"Have you seen Jerusalem? No? Then you have never seen a fine city." That is how people talked in the days of the Great Herod.

It was when this King was rebuilding the temple of Solomon that the strange happening on the Jaffa Sea took place. This sea was not a body of water off by itself. It was really just that part of the vast Mediterranean upon which the city of Jaffa was built. It was at Jaffa's nearby port of Acre that cargoes intended for Jerusalem were landed.

"The Great Herod is rebuilding the temple of Solomon." The word spread far over the ancient Mediterranean world.

"Herod is bringing back its former splendor to the 'House of God' in Jerusalem. It will be once more as magnificent as it was before King Solomon's enemies destroyed it." This was the talk on all the ships in all the harbors of the Great Sea.

Everyone knew of the richness and beauty of this temple which Solomon had built long ago. How thousands of men worked for seven years upon it! How they fitted small, perfect stones cunningly together to make its outer walls! And how rare woods from other lands were carved to adorn it inside! This temple's walls and its altars, and even its floors, were inlaid with pure gold.

Ships once again brought gifts for the temple from far across the sea. Kings and rich merchants of other countries now also were among those who wanted to have a part in the rebuilding of the House of God.

Nikanor was the name of a good Jewish merchant who planned a superb gift for the Great Herod. His home was in the city of Alexandria in Egypt, which lay far across the Mediterranean Sea from Jerusalem. This merchant was so rich that he could well afford to send his temple gift on such a long journey.

"I shall have made for the temple two magnificent doors. They shall be doors fit for the most important entrance in the House of God," Nikanor decided. "They shall be cast in copper. And I shall overlay them with splendid designs of silver and gold."

The finest of copper went into the making of Nikanor's doors. Fifty cubits high they stood. This is to say, they were higher than a five-story house. Forty cubits, or sixty feet, was their width. It took twenty men to lift each door onto the ship that was to take Nikanor's gift across the sea to Acre near the city of Jaffa.

It does not seem strange that the Egyptian merchant should have wanted to go along with his magnificent gift.

During the sea voyage, he scarcely let his treasure out of his sight.

Winds were fair and sailing was smooth during the first part of the journey. But near its end, a storm came. The winds swelled into a tempest. The dark, angry waves mounted until they broke over the ship's masts. They screamed in their fury like demons at war.

The ship's Captain and its crew worked with all their might to keep the vessel afloat under the mountains of water. But at last the Captain gave voice to the fear that was in each sailor's heart.

"It must be that the King of the Sea is angry today. What can we give him out of our cargo to calm his waves? What have we that he would like for his undersea palace?"

They began with the bundles and bales which they could most easily spare. But the storm still raged about their ship. Then the Captain turned to Nikanor.

"One of your temple doors will quiet the Demon of this Sea," he said. "Surely such a door for his palace will please the King of the underwave world."

"One of my doors?" Nikanor could not believe his ears. "Would you throw into this sea my splendid door which is meant for the House of God in Jerusalem? How would you dare to cast away so priceless a treasure?"

"Better that than to have our ship sink! And to have us all drown." The Captain was firm. It was clear he was frightened. For his ship was already sinking low in the sea.

Nikanor stood by, with tears running down his cheeks

while twenty strong sailors heaved one of his precious doors overboard. He moaned aloud when he saw its gold-and-silver beauty swallowed up by the waves.

But the Sea King was still angry. The storm grew even worse.

"One door is not enough for the Sea King. It is surely that he wants both of the doors." The Captain had no pity for poor Nikanor. He thought only that he did not want to lose his ship and his men.

"No! No!" Nikanor climbed onto the second door. "You shall not throw this one into the sea, unless you throw me in with it. This door must somehow reach the Temple of God. Let me be sent down to the Sea Demon in its place as a sacrifice to his anger. But save my door!"

"O God in Heaven," he prayed. "This door for Thy temple is more precious to me than my life. Let me take its place."

Now, it may be that God heard him, and that His great heart was touched so that He Himself calmed the storm. For what happened then was a part of this miracle on the sea.

At once the ocean became calm. Gone were the high winds. As flat as your hand were the waves on that part of the Mediterranean Sea. And the sun shone clear and bright on the gleaming silver and gold of Nikanor's remaining door.

"At least one of my temple doors has been saved," Nikanor comforted himself. But he could not help weeping when he thought of its mate on the bottom of the Great Sea.

It was when the ship was drawing near the Jaffa shore that the great miracle took place. Suddenly a shout came from the sailor in the lookout on the ship's mast.

"The door! The door! Nikanor's door is there, on that wave rolling in to the shore!"

There was wonder in the man's voice. And there was amazement on the faces of Nikanor and the Captain and all on that ship.

For there, floating as easily as though it was a chip of wood, was the massive metal temple door. All could see that it was the very door which had been thrown into the sea during the storm. Openmouthed, they watched it ride the waves gently until it was floated onto the land.

Some said that this was surely another one of God's miracles. Others declared that a giant sea serpent had brought the door to land in its giant jaws. They were sure that the Sea Demon had been touched by Nikanor's unselfish love for his God. They said only a huge sea serpent could have been the Sea King's messenger.

Well, however it was, there the door lay, unharmed on the shore. It was no trouble at all for Nikanor to have it carried, with its mate, over the land to Jerusalem. O, that good merchant was happy when he stood before the Great Herod with his gift for the temple.

Is this story true? You will have to decide that for yourself. But you will find this strange happening described in the Talmud, the Holy Book of the Jews. And it *is* true that through the years many, many pilgrims have admired Nikanor's Doors in Solomon's Temple in Jerusalem.

The Hunting Dog and
the Purple Fish

A MAN AND HIS DOG WERE HUNTING ONE DAY ALONG THE shores of the Mediterranean Sea, near the ancient seaport of Tyre. They were looking for certain sea birds which that man wanted to take home for his supper.

I cannot tell you whether the man killed the sea birds with a hunting knife, or with the short throwing spear called a javelin. Perhaps he used a bow and arrows. Or perhaps he sent tiny stones flying fast through the air from a leather slingshot.

The only thing I can be sure about is that he did not use a gun. For this was long before guns were invented. It was long before Christ was born, in the days when the Mediterranean was the most splendid part of the known world.

The city of Tyre, near which this man lived, was magnificent. And its King was as rich and as powerful as any other in the land.

The story does not tell, either, what kind of a dog that man had. Whether it was a shaggy dog or a dog with a smooth coat, a brown dog or a black dog. It does not really matter.

The important thing is that this dog was a good hunter. Like hunting dogs of today, when his master had brought down a bird out of the air, the dog would run to the place where it had fallen and bring it back to him.

On this day, the sun shone. The air was fresh and the sea birds were many. But for a time the dog was not paying attention to his task of bringing the birds back to his master. There were too many juicy sea creatures for him to eat along the beach. Again and again the dog stopped to dig in the sand, and to sniff at the sea shells scattered upon it.

"Ai! Ai!" the man called to his dog. "Fetch me my bird!" He gave the special command which the dog knew so well. And the animal left off licking the sea shell which he had found. Quicky he ran into the low water to pick up the bird.

Gently holding the sea bird in his jaws, the dog laid it down at his master's feet. When the man bent to pick it up, he saw red water dripping from the dog's mouth. His first thought, of course, was that it was the bird's blood.

But there was no blood at all on the bird's feathers. There was no cut on his body.

That man was fond of his dog, and he gently wiped the

animal's red jaws with a piece of white cloth he had tucked into his hunting robe.

"Perhaps you have cut yourself on the edge of a sharp shell." The man spoke as if the dog could understand him. Then he looked at the dog's mouth.

There was no wound there, either. There was only the dark red color in the animal's watery mouth.

That night, the hunter showed his wife the white cloth with its stain of rich red. And he told her how puzzled he was to find out where it came from.

"I thought it was blood," he explained. "But blood is brown when it dries, and this is still red."

"This stain has a tinge of blue as well as red," his wife replied. "It is the color of the darkest red in the rainbow, where it meets the blue."

"Water will take blood out of cloth," the woman added. "Let me try to wash this red color away." But no matter how many times she put it into water, no matter how hard she scrubbed, its rich crimson hue did not change.

Here, indeed, was a mystery.

"I will watch where our dog goes," the man said to his wife the next time he went hunting. "I must find out from where that strange red color came."

Down on the seashore the animal ran this way and that. He sniffed all the shells that had been washed up by the waves onto the sand.

Suddenly the dog halted. He had found what he wanted,

a pointed shell with rough ridges winding around and around it. Into the shell's curved open side, the dog thrust his tongue. With licking and sucking he drew into his mouth the soft creature that lived in the shell.

Now, a shellfish is not like a swimming fish. Perhaps it is not a true fish at all. For it has no backbone, and it cannot swim.

This was a shellfish of the kind called a mollusk. That is, it had a soft body inside a hard shell. And it was this soft tender body which that hunting dog liked to eat.

When the dog lifted his head at last from his meal, the hunter found the answer to the mystery of the red color. It was the body of the mollusk that turned the animal's tongue, and the water in his mouth, to a deep, deep red.

"Never have I seen a color I like so well," the hunter's wife said when he told her the story that evening. "I will help you gather these mollusks. Together we will take the red from the fish inside their shells. And we will dye beautiful bright cloth for new robes for you and for me."

You can imagine what talk there was in the city of Tyre when the hunter and his wife walked along its streets in their bright crimson robes. You can guess that all the other women, and the men, too, wanted to know whence such a fine color had come.

No doubt that man and his wife grew rich from selling their red dye to those who wanted crimson cloth. But surely the secret of their mollusk hunting could not long be kept.

Soon there must have been others gathering these shells along the Mediterranean shore.

It could not have been very long before the King of Tyre heard of the magnificent dark red robes being worn by his subjects. One look at their rich color, and he wanted such robes for himself and his family. Once he was wearing them, he did not like the idea of lesser people dressing in the robes of a king.

"None but kings and queens and their nobles may wear our Tyrian purple!" he ordered.

He called the new color purple from the name of the mollusk, which in his language was "porphyra." In other countries the rich crimson became "purpura" or "purpel." Of course our own word for it is "purple."

The real Tyrian purple was like a dark red. Little by little, as time went by, more blue was added to the red in the dye. This gave it the color which many purples now have. And of course, in these times of chemical dyes and vegetable colors, the bodies of shellfish are no longer the only place where purple can be found.

In the days of Tyre's splendor, its purple dye was carried on its ships to all parts of the Mediterranean world. Rich jewels, fine glassware, and shining metalwork from Tyre were also in their cargoes. But none of the city's wares brought it more wealth than this precious dye which was discovered by a hunting dog in the body of a "purple" fish.

[253]

The Missing Fog Bell

*A*T ONE PLACE ON THE COAST OF SCOTLAND THERE ARE rocks in the sea as well as on the shore. There are such rocks, too, in other places, but this was in the cove where the fog bell disappeared.

Wherever there are rocks in the sea, fishermen have to keep a sharp lookout. Before they know what is happening, their boats can be thrown by the waves onto those rocks and be dashed to pieces.

The men of this little town on the cove all knew where the rocks were. In the daylight, when the sun shone, they were easy to see. Their wet tops were black amid the white foam of the waves which broke upon them.

But when night had fallen, or when the fog came, aye, then it was bad. Have you ever been out on the sea in a fog? If you have, you know how the thick gray mist hangs like a curtain around your boat. How you can't see from its bow to its stern, much less make out what's in the water ahead.

Now, in this Scottish cove, there was one special rock of which every man out in a boat was afraid. It was only a little way from the cove's entrance. Smaller rocks were near it, and many a boat had been wrecked there.

The stone church of the town was built on the shore, looking down on that rock. The Minister, whom the Scotch folk of the cove called their "Dominie," could see it from his window. And many were the prayers he said about that rock and its danger to his people.

The men and women of that little Scottish town were good church people. Each Sunday they sat in their pews in their "kirk," as they called the church. And they minded the words they heard there. Their Dominie preached a very fine sermon, and everyone looked up to him.

Everyone, that is, except good-for-nothing Jock Burns. As in most other places in the world, here in this fishing town there were a few like Jock Burns who were not so good as their neighbors.

"Jock Burns is the worst one of us all," the townspeople said. Were there nets hung up to dry during the night, and were they gone in the morning? "Look among the nets of good-for-nothing Jock Burns," they said. And the missing nets might well be found there.

Did Jock bring in an extra-full boat of fish? Well, there were hooks on the long lines of other fishermen from which their catch had been taken.

"Jock has made friends with the Devil. The Devil surely

closes our eyes in sleep when Jock steals our nets and our fish." This often was said along the boat landings.

In those early times there was much talk of the Devil around the peat fires on the cottage hearths. And each Sunday morning, in his kirk that looked down on the black rocks, the Dominie warned his people in their pews. "Run from the Devil," he told them. "When the Devil tempts you, run as fast as a sailing ship runs before a strong wind."

This Dominie looked well after the welfare of his people. Did a poor family need food? Somehow he found it for them. Was there a wicked deed done in the town? The Dominie sought out the wrongdoer and begged him to mend his ways.

So it was natural that he often had to seek out Jock Burns. Each time he found him he would plead, "Ah, Jock Burns, will you not mind the way you are going, and leave the Devil behind?

"You can earn a good living, Jock, without stealing and tricks," he would say, "just as your good neighbors do."

That's the way the Dominie talked to this Jock Burns. Kind he was. And his words no doubt troubled the man. For Jock tried to keep out of the Dominie's way.

But the Dominie talked with Jock's wife, and she too got after the man to mend his ways. The scoldings were so bad that Jock Burns was sick and tired of their preaching.

No doubt it was the Devil that put it into Jock's head to get even with the Dominie.

"How shall I bother him most?" Jock Burns said to himself. "I dare not harm the church. I dare not make mischief in the Dominie's cottage. God would punish me surely."

Then he thought of the new fog bell which the Dominie had bought for the cove.

"Our Dominie is a good unselfish man to be caring what happens to the fishing boats." His neighbors said this to Jock when he came home from many days' fishing on the sea. "The Dominie saved his own money to buy us the bell there on the big rock. He says we can hear it ringing far in the fog. It will help us keep our boats well out of the way of the rock."

The people in this town of so long ago did not know much about such bells. Fog bells were new in those times. It was long before there were such things as lighthouses, or beacons, or bell buoys that bobbed up and down in a harbor.

Jock himself scoffed at the idea of a fog bell. He looked at the Dominie's bell chained to a little wood raft anchored beside the dangerous rock. And he said, "If a man is not good enough with his boat to bring it safe home in his own cove, why, let him stay off the sea. No good would the tinkle of this bell be to him."

But the Dominie was pleased with his gift to the town.

"In the fog, you can hear the bell, ringing and ringing. It has a good loud voice," he told the fishermen. "The waves toss its wee raft up and down, and that rings the bell.

Always it rings from its raft by the rock. You can know just where danger lies."

So Jock knew that the fog bell was the way to annoy the Dominie.

It just might not have happened if the first person Jock met on his return from his next fishing trip had not been the Minister of the Kirk. Or if that good man had not asked questions about some nets which had disappeared the day Jock went to sea.

"The Dominie was speaking softly to Jock. But, O, Jock Burns was giving him the Devil's own black looks." That's how the neighbors told of their meeting. And it was that very night that the good-for-nothing man slipped out in a little boat to the wee raft by the rock.

It was a fair, moonlit night. But Jock had no fear of being seen. Every one in his town would be in his bed soon after the sun went down.

It took Jock only a moment to break a link in the chain that held the Dominie's bell fast on its wee raft. And there was a wicked grin on his face when the precious fog bell slid off into the water.

"The Dominie's bell is gone, gone from its wee raft!" The bad news went from cottage to cottage next morning until it came to the Minister. But he would not believe it.

"That bell cannot be gone. It was chained with a fine, strong, iron chain. And there was no storm to break the links of the chain. I will row out and just see for myself."

When his little boat brought him to the side of the black

rock, the Dominie saw at once what had taken place there the night before.

"It was no wave, but a man's tool that broke the link in the chain that held the bell," he reported to his friends on the shore. "Who could have played such a mean trick? Was it you, Sandy? Was it you, Colin?" The Dominie questioned these two who were known for their love of practical jokes.

"It was not me, Dominie."

"Not me, neither, I swear it."

It was clear to everyone that these two were telling the truth.

Then an old man came forward. "It was nobody else but that good-for-nothing Jock Burns," he said. "I saw him myself, creeping out of his house in the moonlight. I watched him go down to the shore and take out his little boat in the middle of the night."

This old man did not sleep so much as when he was young. Often he got out of his bed in the night and looked out at the sea under the stars.

Well, Jock Burns was not in the town on the cove to be questioned that morning. O, no! He was far, far out on the ocean in his big fishing boat.

It was when all the boats were coming home in the evening that the storm came upon them without warning. The sky suddenly grew black. The sea turned a cold gray. Clouds that blew from the northeast brought sheets of rain and a thick blanket of fog.

The fishermen raced for the cove. And just in time, too. For the waves rose higher and higher.

Jock Burns was almost the last to reach the cove. It was dark by then. The fog was so thick that he could not see the top of his boat's mast.

And there was no bell to warn him of the dangerous rock. The man now had good reason to be sorry for his wicked trick of the night before. For his own boat was swept up by the waves and thrown down on the sharp edges of the great black rock. Into more than a hundred pieces it broke. And Jock Burns found himself swimming around and around in the fog-covered water?

It may have been a miracle. Or it may have been the prayers of the Dominie, who begged the good Lord to keep his people on the sea safe. However it was, Jock Burns was washed up by the waves into the very last of the fishing boats that found its way home through the fog.

Jock himself said he deserved to lose his boat on the rock. And that was a curious way for this man to speak. All his neighbors said so.

It is strange what will sometimes turn a bad man into a good one. Out there in the fog, swimming for his life, Jock Burns must have thought of the good Dominie and been sorry. For the very next morning he asked pardon for throwing the fog bell into the ocean. And, of course, the Dominie had to forgive him.

How long it was before the townspeople could save enough money to replace the Dominie's fog bell, I cannot

tell you. But I do know that, today, in almost every harbor
on that Scottish coast, there are bells bobbing up and down
in the water. Like the Dominie's bell, they warn seamen
of dangerous rocks or reefs so that they can keep well away
from them in a fog.

The Three Waves

On SUNDAYS THE FRENCH BASQUE BOY, MANESH, SAT with the men in one of the galleries along the walls of the stone church. He was proud that he was old enough to leave his mother and sister in the place kept for the women and girls on the church floor.

Manesh liked it best when his grandfather would lead him to the very highest gallery. Up there he was closest to the tiny ship model which hung from a hook in the center of the church roof. The boy liked to watch the little ship twist and turn on its long cord. It moved with each draft of air that blew in around the high windows.

The boy's fisherman father often stopped in at the church also on weekdays. He wanted to see which way the ship model was turning before he put his boat into the water.

"You can tell what the weather is going to be by watching the little ship," he told Manesh.

There was something about the dampness in the air which changed the ship model's movements. But Manesh, himself, could never remember just what to look for to foretell stormy weather.

"Why does that little ship hang in our church, Amatchi?*" Manesh had asked his grandmother when he was much smaller.

"To remind us to pray for our men on the sea," the old woman had replied. "We say prayers each Sunday for those who go out in the fishing boats. People have said them here for hundreds of years. And for hundreds of years a small ship has hung above our heads so that we shall not forget."

"Long, long ago," his grandmother reminded the boy, "we French Basques took bigger fish out of the sea than we do today. Our men even caught whales. And big fish are far more exciting than the little herring they bring back now to the cannery.

"It was more dangerous then, too. We have the same sudden storms on our Bay of Biscay. But long ago there were more water witches and demons. My own grandfather told me this was so. And he knew, for he, also, was a fisherman all his life long."

In his high gallery, with his eyes fixed on the gently turning small ship, Manesh sometimes forgot to listen to the words of the good priest far below him. He thought

---

*The Basque name for grandmother.

[268]

instead of his father and his older brother, who were even then out on the sea on a long fishing trip.

The Basque boy could not help imagining the terrible things that might be happening to them. The tempest that might overturn their boat! The wind that might tear its sails! And the water demons and witches! Who could be sure they were all gone from the ocean?

There often came to his mind a story which Aitatchi,* his grandfather, told him while they were mending the fishing nets. "The Three Waves," it was called. And it went like this.

In the long-ago time, there was a Basque fishing boat which sailed every day out of the Bay of Biscay into the Atlantic Ocean. And working on that boat there was a lad who was not more than fifteen years old, Bilinch by name.

The fishermen on this boat were all good at the oars and quick with the sails. The boat itself was one of the best that set forth from the little port of Socoa, near the town of Saint Jean de Luz.

Always it would be first to arrive at the fishing grounds. One would have thought it would bring home the most fish. And so it did, until one year when no fish at all swam into its nets.

"Bad luck rides with us," the Captain said to his crew. "We have the best boat on the ocean. We use the strongest

*The Basque word for Grandfather.

nets. And yet we catch nothing." The men looked at each other with puzzled eyes.

One night Bilinch and the Captain were busy making the boat ready for its early start the next morning. They were to spend the night on the boat. And when all was in order, they lay down to sleep.

It was midnight, and the stars were bright overhead, when Bilinch gave a loud cry. "Did you see them, Captain? Did you hear them? Two sea witches were here. I saw them plainly."

"Go back to sleep, Boy." The Captain only half opened his eyes. "You've had a nightmare. You can see now there is no one, no one at all, here on our boat. Go back to sleep."

But when the morning sky showed pink, and the rest of the crew were aboard, Bilinch fell on his knees at the feet of the Captain.

"Please let me stay home today, my Captain," he cried. "I cannot go out on the ocean today. O, do not make me go." The boy's face was white with his fear.

"Why not, Bilinch? Why not?" The Captain demanded.

"I cannot go. O, I cannot go." This was all the boy would say, but he said it over and over.

"You hired yourself to me for the season. You promised you would work with us every day," the Captain insisted. "Unless you have a good reason, you must come with us."

"It is because trouble waits for us on the ocean today,"

Bilinch declared. "We shall all drown. But I dare not mention the name of the one who told me so."

"Well, we shall have to run that risk. Danger waits for this boat every day it puts out to sea." The Captain spoke sternly. "Perhaps you mean this as a joke, Boy. But I have no time for tricks. Push off, my men! Run up the sails and let us be gone! We are already late."

All the way out of the harbor, Bilinch protested. The row of houses on the Socoa waterfront soon faded into the distance. And they were out on the open sea.

Then the boy's fear of the ocean grew greater than his fear of speaking of the sea witches.

"I will tell the reason, my Captain," he cried. "Last night while you slept, I was wakened by the noise of women's skirts brushing against the side of the boat. I opened my eyes. And I swear I saw the forms of the two witches I told you about.

"In the bright starlight I saw them clearly. And, O, I was frightened. I was so frightened I could not move. I scarcely breathed, and that saved me. For those sea witches thought that, like you, I was asleep.

"The witches danced on our boat. They sang a horrid song. Then I felt our boat rise up into the air. High above the water they lifted it. And far, far across the sky they carried it until it was caught and held in the branches of an old olive tree."

The sailors laughed then. "What a dream!" they cried. "A boat up in an olive tree!" And they laughed some more.

But they did not laugh so heartily when Bilinch showed them the twig he had broken off that olive tree in the night. They listened in silence while he told how the witches brought the boat back to its home landing. There was fear in their faces, too, when he repeated the words he had heard the witches speak to each other.

"You can bid the Captain and his boy good-by, my daughter," he heard the older witch say. "Never again shall they sail the sea after this day. Two hours hence their boat will be down, down under the waves, on the sea bottom."

"But the wind is fair today, Mother? The ocean is calm."

"All the same, this is the last journey for those who ride in this boat. I shall send my three waves upon them—my wave white as milk, my wave clear as tears, and, yes, my wave red as blood. How shall any boat come through my three waves?"

"Why do you want to destroy the men of this boat, Mother?"

"They have offended the Sea King," the older witch answered. "How I do not know. Perhaps they have been too bold on the sea. Or too proud. But he is angry. It was at his command that I have kept the fish out of their nets. Now it is his will that they must drown. If it does not happen today, the Sea Demon will be forced to leave them alone."

"And is there no way for them to escape, Mother?" The younger witch had seemed sorry for those in Bilinch's boat.

"There is one way, indeed. But how shall they find it? This boat may ride safely over my first wave, the wave white as milk. This boat may come through my second wave, the wave clear as tears. But no boat can escape my wave, red as blood, unless the harpoon is thrown into it. That blood-red wave will be myself. Its heart will be my heart. Let the harpoon reach my heart and I shall die. And the men in this boat will be saved.

"But there is no danger that these men shall learn my secret. You, my daughter, and I are the only ones in the whole world who could tell it to them."

"So, my Captain, turn back. I pray, turn back." Bilinch was again kneeling at his master's feet.

"Aye Master, let us turn back," the sailors cried, too. "There is no olive tree near the landing where our boat lay last night. We believe the boy's story."

But the bold Captain stood firm.

"We shall fish as usual today," he cried to the crew. Then, to calm their fears, he added, "But we shall be ready for the sea witch and her three waves." He put the strongest of the sailors with the harpoon into the very bow of the boat. He himself kept watch for the coming of the witch's three waves.

Smooth as glass was the sea that day. Fair was the wind in the boat's sails. But there was no laughing or joking among the sailors who sat ready with their hands on the oars. If the three waves came, surely they would need oars as well as sails to ride safely over them.

"The wave white as milk!" It was Bilinch who first saw the mass of white water rise out of the calm ocean.

"O, the wave white as milk!" the others shouted. And they worked with the sails and bent to the oars with all their might. So strong were these men that the boat rode safely over the milky white wave.

It was but a few moments before they saw rushing towards them a wave even higher. Like a crystal mountain it seemed, with no more color than tears.

"The wave clear as tears!" Bilinch shouted.

"O, the wave clear as tears!" the crew echoed his cry. And they bent to their work. They steadied the boat and they kept it right side up, such good boatmen were they.

A hot mist rose from this crystal wave. It made their eyes smart, but the men did not leave their posts until the boat had won its way through to the calm water beyond.

Hardly had they time for a rest when the worst happened. In front of their fishing boat there was lifted out of the ocean a giant wave of bright red. Some might have thought that its color came from the rising sun. But Bilinch knew better.

"The wave red as blood, Master," he called. "The wave red as blood!"

"The harpoon! Throw the harpoon!" The Captain gave the order just in time. With a mighty thrust, the man in the bow sent his barbed weapon into the very heart of the red wave.

A groan like the thunder sounded over the sea. The wave

split in two. Its red foam spurted high and far to either side. A whirlpool was formed, and Bilinch declared he saw the head of the sea witch in its center.

"Bilinch! Bilinch! Long live Bilinch, who saved us from the three waves!" All the men on that boat shouted praise of the lad.

The rest of that day they were busy taking the fish out of their nets. They had scarcely room enough in their boat to take home all they caught. And they were large, fine fish. Such a good catch they made in that one day that it wiped from their minds the bad luck which had gone before.

The Bride from the Sea

*H*AVE YOU EVER SEEN A MERMAID, GRANDFATHER?"
Jeannie looked up from her wooden stool at the old fisherman's side.

The two, the old man and the little girl, were busy at
work just outside their cottage door. They were mending
a net which the fishermen of their family would use the
next day. The herring were running in the northern waters
off their rocky Shetland Island. Each morning the boats of
the Scotch fishermen who lived on it went forth to make
their catch.

"A mermaid is it you ask about, Lassie?" The clear blue
eyes twinkled in the ruddy wrinkled face of the old fisherman. "Well, now, I cannot say truly that I've seen a mermaid. But I've seen many a seal playing amid the rocks off
our isles. And who can say that one of these pretty creatures

is not a mermaid. The water lassies often put on the skin of a seal when they come close to land."

"A seal's skin would be a good covering for a mermaid." Jeannie nodded her head. "A seal's head is about the same size. A seal's flippers are just about as long as her arms would be. Aye, Grandfather, a mermaid could easily hide herself in a seal's skin."

This Scotch girl, on her rocky Shetland Isle, liked to hear her grandfather tell stories about the sea people who live under the waves. Perhaps she did not quite believe them all. But who could be sure they were not true, after all?

Jeannie often thought about the sea. She liked to stand on a cliff and watch the great waves that came rolling up to her island. It was exciting to see them break over the rocks in clouds of white spray.

Where did the waves come from, she wondered? What did they say? She could hear their loud roar before they dashed themselves against the shore.

What was there beneath those waves? Men talked of sea serpents and even of demons. Why then should there not be sea men and sea maids who lived, like the seals, in that underwave world?

"I had it from my grandsire. And he had it from his grandsire." Jeannie's grandfather nodded his head wisely as he quoted his ancestors. "Truly there are sea people. There are good ones and bad ones, just like people on the land. The good mermaids make fine wives for young men. And the bad ones?" Here he shook his white head. "The bad

ones are to be left alone. Their sweet songs have led sailors
onto the sharp rocks and drowned them in the sea."

Jeannie enjoyed most the stories about sea maids who
once married young fishermen and lived on the land. She
wished she might, one day, see these sea brides throw off
their sealskins and dance on the shore.

One such tale which this Scottish girl specially liked is
this one I am setting down here for you.

Long, long ago, on a moonlight night, a young fisherman
walked along a sheltered cove not far from his home. As
he rounded a rocky point, he spied a band of handsome
young people dancing on its sandy beach.

"Sea people they must be. Sea men and sea maids!" he
said in surprise. And he dropped down behind a rock to
watch them in their dance.

The young men were handsome, and the sea maids
were fair. They looked not a bit different than that young
fisherman's own friends in the cove village. Only, these
boys and girls from the ocean were more graceful as they
danced.

"The sea people have left off their sealskins. There they
are, piled on the edge of the beach." The young man was
so excited that he spoke out loud. Of course, no one heard
him but himself.

"There is one small skin quite near my rock," he continued. "I'll play a fine trick. I'll hide one skin well away in
these rocks. Then I'll see what will happen."

Softly he crept out of his hiding place. When he darted to pick up the sealskin nearby, his feet made no sound on the soft sand. But when he ran back again, he stepped upon a large shell. The dancers heard the sharp sound of the shell's breaking. They looked around just in time to see the young man disappearing behind his rock.

With soft, frightened cries, like the barking of seals, they ran to put on their skin coverings. Scrambling together, they rushed to the ocean's edge and dived under the waves.

All disappeared except one. That one was a fair sea maid who ran hither and thither, looking for her sealskin. Without it, of course she could not go back into the sea.

Even while this girl wept, she was the most beautiful maid that the young fisherman had ever seen. Straightway he fell deeply in love with her.

"Help me, Man! Help me!" the sea maiden begged, when the fisherman came from behind the big rock to comfort her. When the sea people have their human forms, it seems they are able to use human speech.

"Help me find my lost sealskin, Young Man, I beg you. Without my sealskin to cover me, I may not go back to my home in the sea." O, she was sad, but the young man loved her so much that he did not want her to leave him. He wanted her for his wife.

"I do not see your sealskin, my Lass." This much was true. And he had not said that he did not know where it was. So he did not really lie to her. But neither did he tell her that he himself had hidden it under a rock.

"Stay here with me on the land, dear Lass," he said to the mermaid. "I will make you my bride. I will love you and care for you all your life long. We'll be happy together in my cottage on the cove."

Well, the young fisherman was handsome. And he seemed to be kind. What could that mermaid do but go with him to his snug cottage on the seashore?

Perhaps she fell a little in love with the young fisherman, too. However it was, she made him a good wife. And there were born to them two children, a fine boy and a fair girl.

But the sea bride was not happy. That was plain for her husband to see, and it made him sad. O, she loved her children and she loved her husband too. But each day she went down to the beach where he had found her. Amid the rocks, she stood looking and looking across the wide water. And each day she searched and she searched for her lost sealskin.

"Perhaps I should tell my dear wife where her sealskin is hidden," the fisherman said to himself again and again. "But there, on the edge of the ocean, I see her talking to the seals which swim close in to the shore. She would surely go off with them. And I should be left alone." He loved his bride from the sea so much that he never showed her the hiding place of her precious skin.

Sometimes he begged the sea maid to try to be happy. "You do not love me as I love you," he cried, "or you would not be so sad."

"I love you truly," the sea bride replied. "But the ocean

is my home. It is there, under the waves, that I belong. If I could but find my sealskin again, I could go back."

So you see, it was not that the sea bride did not love her land family. It was just that her longing for the sea was so strong that she forgot everything else. Jeannie and her grandfather understood how this might be. They too loved the ocean. They were sorry for people who never sniffed the tangy smell of salt water, nor felt the sting of the ocean spray on their faces.

It was the sea bride's young son who brought the sealskin back to her at last. One day he and his sister were playing on the rocks by the seashore. And the boy spied a bit of sealskin sticking out from between two rocks. He ran gaily to show his treasure to his mother, who was wading in the low water.

"Look, Mother, look! I have found a fine sealskin!" The boy was excited.

But his mother was more excited than he. She snatched the sealskin quickly out of his hands. Then she fairly danced for joy. The boy told his father how it was that night at their supper.

"My mother laughed and she sang. She forgot all about us children when she put on that sealskin. O, she looked just like a seal when she dived into the ocean. And she did not come out again."

The two children cried for their mother. Perhaps their father found a kind village woman to cook their food and mend their clothes. But the boy and the girl often went down to the rocks and looked out to sea. They were hoping and hoping that their own dear mother would come back to them.

And perhaps she did. For one gentle seal swam often into that cove. Out of the waves she would rise, holding her round head high and stretching her sleek neck. Surely this was their mother. It was plain that she was looking to see that all was well with her children.

Whenever the fisherman's son and daughter saw this particular seal, they cried aloud, "Put off your sealskin, dear Mother! Come back! O, come back and be our mother again!"

But she never did.